G000058600

To my lovely son, who is possibly the best cook I've ever met. Thank you for taking care of me the last few months. If I could employ you to cook me forever I would.

1

PJ

PJ stared moodily into his hot chocolate, the ends of his untidy beard almost dipping into the hot drink. He barely noticed. PJ had made his mom's recipe, just as they always had, but it wasn't the same as Lyle's. Gruff's boy just made it better. But Gruff and Lyle were thousands of miles away, saving the world, and he was stuck here, on the farm, staring into a cup of hot chocolate.

The kitchen door opened and Harry, his older brother, stomped in, taking off his hat to reveal an untidy mop of copper hair. "It's cold out there. Thunder is sulking. Be careful if you go near him."

"Why would I be stupid enough to go near Thunder," PJ grumbled.

Thunder was his oldest brother's horse. They had the same temperament, growly and moody.

"What's your problem?" Harry snapped.

PJ didn't respond and Harry sighed, squeezing PJ's shoulder. "I know, I know. I miss them too, little brother."

"We should be with them," PJ said, leaning into his brother's comfort. He missed the bickering and the scuffles, the banter around the kitchen table. He missed Damien's grumpiness and Gruff going all Daddy Bear when he thought anyone was rude to his boy. Not that any of the brothers would dare to be rude to Lyle who took such good care of them.

"No, they should be here, with us." Harry gave one tight squeeze, then went to the stove to peer into the hot chocolate pan. He made a satisfied sound as he ladled two spoons into a cup with blue and white stripes.

Harry sat down at the table. PJ wanted to have his sulk in peace, but he knew Harry was struggling as much as he was. At least Harry had the horses to keep him company. PJ only had the trees. Not that he hadn't hugged one or two trees since his brothers went on the road.

"They'll be back soon, bro," Harry said, breaking into his thoughts.

PJ gave him a hangdog expression. "When? It's been a month and there's no sign of them coming back yet. Damien said Florida was awful. He's had to bring Vinny off the ledge."

"I know. He called me too."

PJ's lips twitched. "How many times has he called you today?"

"Two times before breakfast." Harry smirked at PJ. "And one more when he pretended he butt-dialed me."

"Me too."

"He's struggling worse than we are. Even Lyle's called once a day to see what we're eating."

PJ chuckled. "I swear that boy thinks we never cooked for ourselves before he arrived."

"I miss his cooking," Harry admitted.

"Me too. Even Mom's meatloaf wasn't as good as his. Not that I'd ever have told her if she were here," PJ added hastily. No one ever criticized their late mom without the other brothers falling on them like a ton of bricks.

Harry patted his hand. "I know what you mean. Mom would have loved Lyle. Especially as she didn't like cooking."

PJ furrowed his brow. "Mom loved cooking."

"Mom loved *us*," Harry contradicted. "Cooking for the family came with the territory."

"Wow, I never knew that."

"You were never in the kitchen long enough to find out."

It wasn't a criticism. PJ knew that. He'd always been the one by his dad's and Damien's side, running the farm. He'd always been closer to his dad than his mom. But PJ was feeling vulnerable today and the comment stung. He didn't want a fight with his brother though and he knew Harry meant well. "I miss Lyle's hot chocolate. It's always better than mine."

"Yours is fine but sometimes Lyle puts a pinch of chili in it," Harry said. "That's what gives it the bite."

"I've gotta spend more time in the kitchen," PJ muttered.

"You're doing just fine."

Now there was only Brad, Harry and him, PJ was the younger brother, and PJ had a feeling Harry needed to take care of him just to make himself feel better.

"Where's Brad?" PJ asked.

"Where do you think? He's in the barn."

PJ rolled his eyes. "There's nothing left to blow up."

"Brad can always find something to blow up," Harry

pointed out. "But he's making repairs to the back wall of the barn. The last explosion went wrong."

All the brothers had their interests. Brad loved explosions.

Harry smirked across the table. "Did you hear he's been offered a book deal? A publisher read his poems and wants to publish them."

Explosions and poetry. It was a combination PJ couldn't get his head around. PJ was a guy with simple needs. A boy across his lap and a good IPA.

PJ stared at Harry. "You're joking."

Harry shook his head. "I'm not. Our brother is going to be a published poet."

"Grief," PJ muttered. He drained his cup and took it to the sink to rinse out. "I'm going into town to get supplies. Do you need anything?"

"I need toothpaste."

"Done." PJ didn't really need supplies. He just wanted to get away from the cabin. He felt as if the walls were closing in on him, even when he was outside.

Harry leaned back in his chair and looked up at his younger brother. "What about a trip to the Tin Bar tomorrow? It's been a month since the Brenner boys went in there to cause trouble."

PJ almost said no. Tomorrow was Tuesday. Daddies and boys night. But Jake wasn't there and he was the one who caused the most trouble. PJ shook his head to dislodge his gloomy thoughts. He needed to quit feeling sorry for himself and just enjoy a night out at the bar. "Yeah, why not," he agreed. "I could do with spanking a sweet boy's ass." There was a cute blond who always made a beeline for PJ. Sadly PJ didn't feel any spark for him, but he was happy to take care of the kid while he was there.

"Just make sure it's not that kid who tried to cause trouble for Jake. What was his name?"

"I don't think we ever found out," PJ said. "But I remember who he is. That kid deserves time out in the corner—permanently."

"He does," Harry agreed. "Still, if the brat hadn't caused trouble, Jake and Aaron would still be mooning at each other."

"Tomorrow we go to the Tin Bar and drag Brad with us."

Harry nodded. "Deal."

PJ headed to the hall to put on his jacket and boots. He would get the supplies, then go to the diner for a late lunch and a chance to catch up with his friend, Sheila.

"Brush your hair," Harry yelled from the kitchen as PJ opened the door.

PJ growled under his breath.

"Dollar."

"Later," PJ growled.

Like Harry had heard him. He was going to buy feed, not go on a date. But he stepped into the bathroom and quickly combed his hair, not that it made a lot of difference. PJ was way past due for Brad to give him a trim and tidy up his beard.

He stepped outside and raised his face to catch the late spring sunshine. He inhaled the sweet air and slowly exhaled. This was a good idea. He needed a break from the cabin.

PJ took a slow drive down the mountain road, windows down, blasting out country and western. His brothers mocked him unmercifully for his choices, but he loved it and didn't care who knew.

Buying the supplies took five minutes and he remem-

bered Harry's toothpaste as he reached the truck. PJ was
tempted to pretend he'd forgotten but he knew Harry
would give him a hard time. He returned to the store and
purchased the toothpaste, along with a bright pink tooth-
brush because he was an ass, then got in the truck to head
to the diner.

The parking lot was half-empty, but the diner seemed
full. Sheila scurried between the tables as he walked in.

PJ waved at her. "Hey, gorgeous, you're looking real
pretty today."

Sheila came over and he bent so she could kiss him on
the cheek. "Afternoon, PJ. On your own today?"

"Yep."

"How're you doing?" She patted his back, her eyes
sympathetic.

"Not good," he confessed. Sheila had known the family
for years and knew how close the brothers were. She
wouldn't laugh at a big guy like PJ missing his family. "I
want to eat my weight in pancakes to forget."

She pointed him to a booth. "I'll be over in a moment
with the coffee pot, hun."

PJ walked through the diner, waving at a few people he
knew, rolling his eyes at the couple who blanked him. There
were a few people who disapproved of his family. Seven gay
boys was all wrong. He'd heard the whispered comments
about not being brought up right. But his mom and dad
had loved them all fiercely. PJ gave the couple the biggest
smile he could. As far as he was concerned, folks who
disapproved of them could take a one-way ticket on the
next bus out of town.

He saw one face he didn't know, tucked into a booth as
if he were hiding. A young sandy-haired man, barely older

than Lyle or Vinny. He looked tired, his shoulders slumped, as he drank a cup of coffee.

"Who's the kid?" PJ murmured when Sheila came over with the coffee pot.

"Came in on the bus," she said. "Never seen him before."

She topped off his coffee and vanished toward the kitchen, returning a few minutes later with a plate piled high with pancakes and an equally large stack of bacon. He saw the boy glance over, then quickly look away as PJ caught his eye. He was still just drinking coffee, no food in front of him.

PJ finished his lunch and glanced at his phone. It was time to make his way home. Sheila wasn't anywhere to be seen, so he headed over to the counter to settle the check. He'd pay for the kid to get a hot meal inside him too.

"Excuse me."

He turned, but as he did swung his arm out. To his horror, it connected with the blond boy. PJ was sure it was only a tap, but the kid collapsed, poleaxed, to the ground, and his head hit the ground with a sickening thud.

"What the heck, PJ?" Sheila yelled, rushing around the counter.

PJ knelt by the unconscious kid. "I hit him."

"I can see that, mountain man," she snapped. "The question is, why?"

If PJ knew that he wouldn't have done it. "I didn't do it deliberately. You know I'm a klutz and he was kinda in the way." He stroked the boy's hair away from his face, noting the creamy skin and long eyelashes fanning his cheeks. The boy had a light spray of freckles across his nose. He sure was a pretty one, but too pale. "Hey there, little one, time to wake up."

JACK

Jack tried to open his eyes at the order from the deep, growly voice, but they really didn't want to cooperate. "Daddy?"

He felt, rather than heard rumbling beneath his cheek. That was strange. Was it an earthquake? Had he been knocked out in a shockwave? He hadn't been in an earthquake before. And why did his cheek hurt so much? Was he lying on the ground? It was very soft and warm, and it smelled of pine and dirt, and something deeper and richer. Jack wanted to stay where he was and inhale it.

"Not yet, boy." Was that amusement? What was funny? What had Jack said?

Jack touched his face. "Hurts."

"You'll be fine once we get an ice pack on it."

"Do you want me to call an ambulance, PJ?" A concerned female voice.

Jack struggled but it was as if he were pinned down. "Can't go to hospital."

"Hush, quit struggling, boy," PJ—Jack assumed it was PJ —ordered. As Jack subsided, a huge hand cupped his jaw and something cold was pressed to his cheek. "He'll be fine, Sheila. I'll take care of him. I owe him that. Just add his order to mine and I'll pay it."

"He only had coffee. He can have that on the house. I don't think the kid's got any money," Sheila said.

Jack's cheeks burned with embarrassment as he listened to them talk above him. She was right. He didn't have a cent to his name. The last thing he remembered was working up the nerve to ask for a job in a diner.

He whimpered and PJ hushed him again. "Good boy.

I'm gonna take you home and Harry can check you out. Not that he's gonna believe what just happened."

Jack was confused. Who was Harry? But he was very tired and when the world moved, he hung on tight in case it was another shockwave. "I haven't got any money. Don't hurt me."

A deep sigh. "I already did that, kid. Just open your eyes so I know you don't think I'm kidnapping you."

Jack wanted to obey the order, he really did. PJ was gentle with his orders and he liked that. He struggled to open his eyes. Finally he cracked one eye open to look into the deepest blue eyes he'd ever seen, and a beard that seem to go on forever. Jack licked his lips. "Was there an earthquake?"

PJ gave a wry smile. "No, sweetheart, not an earthquake. I hit you."

Furrowing his brow hurt like hell, but he was sure PJ just said he hit Jack. That didn't make sense. "Why did you hit me?"

"It wasn't intentional." PJ gave him an apologetic smile. "I turned, swung my arm out by accident, and you were there."

"I was at a diner."

"You're still here. I'm gonna take you home, little one."

Jack liked being called little one, but he was sure that he shouldn't be called a pet name by a complete stranger. He was a man, after all. But PJ stood, holding Jack as though he weighed nothing and hugged Jack to his chest.

"My name's Jack." It seemed important he told PJ his name.

"Good to meet you, Jack. I'm PJ," the big man rumbled. "Paul Joseph Brenner, but everyone calls me PJ."

Jack didn't feel any need to give his last name. He didn't

need to be laughed at by strangers. "I need to find somewhere to sleep before it gets dark." The temperature had plummeted, and it was too cold to sleep outside. He'd planned to find a job, then somewhere to stay. Getting knocked unconscious had not been on his things-to-do list. He didn't even know what time it was.

"You can stay at the cabin tonight. There's plenty of room."

Jack thought PJ looked sad about that. "The cabin?"

"My home. My family own a Christmas tree farm up the mountain. Offering you a bed for the night is the least I can do, little one. Can you put your hand in my top pocket for my wallet?"

Jack did as he asked, trying not to grope the heavy pec at the same time.

PJ looked over his shoulder. "Sheila, can I settle the check?"

"Sure thing, hun." Sheila came over and took the wallet from Jack as if she'd done it before.

"Add in Jack's coffee and your usual tip," PJ said.

"You're a good boy," Sheila cooed, taking the notes, and handing the wallet back to Jack, who returned it to PJ's pocket.

Then they were out in the cold night air and heading to an old truck.

PJ said, "Could you get my keys? Same pocket."

"Are you sure you don't want me to just feel you up?" Jack quipped as he pulled out the keys.

It was meant to be light-hearted, but he saw the sudden heat and intensity in PJ's eyes. The big man liked that idea. Jack sucked in a breath at the sudden thought of caressing PJ.

"Maybe when I've not tried to knock you unconscious," PJ suggested.

He put Jack on the ground and any thought of flirting went right out of Jack's head as his stomach and head spun in opposite directions. Jack clutched onto PJ for support.

"Are you gonna barf?" PJ asked.

"Not sure yet," Jack said through gritted teeth. It was fifty-fifty whether he was going to vomit or pass out again.

"Lean against me," PJ crooned.

Jack did as he suggested, which only made him realize just how tall PJ was. He barely came up to PJ's chest. "Jeez, you're a giant."

PJ gave a rumbling laugh. "I am. Nearly seven foot tall."

"Did your mom stick you in a grow bag?" Jack grumbled. He'd always been sensitive about his height.

"She bore tall men," PJ said. "Do you feel well enough to get in the truck?"

Jack wasn't sure but they couldn't stay in the parking lot for the rest of the day. "I do."

PJ barked out a laugh. "Oh baby, you're getting ahead of yourself. We've only just met."

"Huh?" Then Jack realized what he'd just said. He felt his cheeks heat. "You're an ass."

"It's been said before," PJ said easily as he helped Jack into the van. "But just to warn you. We've got a strict no cussing policy at home. It's a dollar a word."

Jack stared at him in horror. "I haven't got any money."

"It's okay. We're responsible for our boys."

PJ shut the door on Jack's confused "But I'm not your boy."

Jack chewed on his lip as PJ drove out of the parking lot. PJ was throwing out 'boy' like candy. Did he understand what he was saying, or did he call everyone his boy? Jack didn't know much about Daddies, but he knew they liked saying 'boy' and being all growly and barking out orders. Just like PJ.

He hadn't seen much of the town when he arrived as he'd been starving and headed straight for the diner. He was still hungry, and his belly grumbled, as if it agreed.

PJ chuckled. "I guess I didn't give you a chance to eat, huh?"

"No." Jack glanced out of the window. "I was gonna ask if I could work in payment for a meal."

"Sheila would have fed you, boy. She's kind like that. But what are you going to do with no money in your pocket?"

"I need to find a job."

"This is a small town," PJ said. "There aren't many jobs here. You should have stayed on the bus until the city."

"This was as far as I could afford," Jack admitted.

"Are you running away from something or someone?" PJ asked kindly.

Jack turned to look at him. "Are you psychic?"

PJ gave another chuckle and Jack noticed how easily he laughed. Jack couldn't remember the last time he'd laughed at anything.

"It's a thing in our family. You're number four," PJ said.

That made no sense to Jack, but PJ didn't seem to want to elaborate further.

"Are you married?" Jack asked.

"Hell no." PJ seemed highly amused by the idea.

"You said Harry would check me over."

"Harry is my brother. There's also another brother, Brad, at home. I have four other brothers but they're away from home at the moment."

"Wow. You've got a big family." Jack blinked at the idea

of seven brothers. Were they all as big as PJ? "I don't have any siblings."

"Do you have any family?" At Jack's hesitation, PJ patted his leg. "You don't have to tell me."

"I have my gran and an uncle," Jack said reluctantly.

"Are you running away from them? Did they hurt you?"

Jack pressed his lips together and looked out of the window. "No, they didn't hurt me."

Yet.

To his surprise, PJ didn't press him for more information, or tell him to go back to his family.

"Well, if you're going to stand on your own two feet, little man, you need a job, somewhere to live, and money in your pocket."

"I was trying to sort that out before you hit me," Jack pointed out, getting tired of the 'little man' crack. He might be short compared to the man mountain next to him, but it didn't mean he was incapable of taking care of himself. The lack of money, job, and home didn't help.

"You're right," PJ said cheerfully. "I'm sorry. Let me help you as I was an ass. You stay with us tonight and tomorrow we'll find you a job and somewhere to stay."

Jack swallowed back the bitter taste of disappointment. PJ didn't want him to be his boy. He was just being kind. He looked out the window at the darkening afternoon. He mustn't be greedy. Jack slipped his hand into his pocket and wrapped it around his most precious possession, taking comfort from it. Not everyone knew how to be a Daddy.

2

PJ

Harry blinked as PJ led Jack into the kitchen. "At least this one walked in," he muttered.

"This is Jack. He was unconscious for a short while," PJ explained. "I hit him."

"Trust you to do that." Harry looked at PJ who nodded to give permission.

PJ decided not to explain it to Jack just yet. The boy seemed too out of it to care.

Harry eased Jack into a chair by the pine table and examined the bump on Jack's head. PJ hovered anxiously until Harry scowled at him.

"Back away, kid. You're making Jack nervous." Harry turned back to Jack. "Sorry for my kid brother. He's got no manners."

PJ growled at the kid brother crack, but he left them alone and occupied himself making a new pan of hot chocolate. He poured a large cup for Jack and handed it to him when Harry was done. Jack stared at it in disbelief, reminding PJ of Lyle when he realized he wasn't going to be starved.

"You're fine, kid," Harry said. "From the color of your face, you look like you need a good meal inside you."

"Yeah, he does," PJ agreed.

"I'm not a kid," Jack muttered. "I'm twenty-two."

With blond hair and baby blue eyes, PJ would have put Jack at eighteen, tops. He probably didn't have to shave more than once a week.

Jack seemed to notice PJ's and Harry's skeptical expressions. "I can show you my ID."

"Yeah, that doesn't work for us. The last kid told us he was twenty-five and showed us his ID. He turned out to be nineteen," PJ said.

"Last kid?" Jack asked. He didn't seem happy with the idea.

"You're number four."

"Great. Now it sounds like we're trafficking boys," Harry said.

Jack blinked at him. "I don't understand."

PJ looked at Harry who just shrugged. "Thanks," he muttered. "That's a lot of help."

"He's gonna find out sooner or later," Harry pointed out. "It's up to you when you decide to tell him."

"Tell me what?" Jack demanded. "Why am I number four? Do you make a habit of taking kids off the streets?"

"I suppose we do, but not for the reason you're thinking." PJ sat down next to Jack. "We're all gay. All seven brothers."

Jack's eyes widened. "You're kidding me, right?"

PJ shook his head. "Do you have a problem with that?"

Much as he wanted to help the kid, if Jack had a

problem with them being gay, PJ could drive him back to town and get him a room at the motel.

"I'm gay too," Jack muttered.

PJ let out a breath. One crisis averted.

"You may as well tell him the rest of it," Harry said.

PJ scowled at his brother. "Haven't you got something useful to be doing?"

Harry gave him a blank stare. PJ huffed and turned back to Jack.

"Listen, kid, we're all Daddies too." He saw Jack's eyes widen almost comically. "Do you even know what I'm talking about?"

"I know," Jack said. "But seven gay Daddies living in one house?"

PJ looked at Jack. Was that a hint of excitement in his voice? "Damien, Jake, Alec, and Gruff have found their boys."

"They brought them home unconscious too," Harry pointed out helpfully.

PJ threw his hands up in the air, nearly smacking Jack again.

"Watch it!" Jack almost fell backward as he tried to get away from PJ's flailing hands. "You make a habit of this?"

PJ took a deep breath. "Harry, get lost."

Harry stood and grinned at Jack. "You're fine, kid. Just be careful of standing in the way of man mountain here."

He disappeared with a chuckle, leaving PJ with a scowling Jack.

"It's not like it sounds," PJ started. He stopped and tried again. "Well, it *is* like it sounds. Gruff found Lyle unconscious in our woods and brought him home. Damien took care of Vinny. At least he walked into the house. Jake found Aaron passed out in the road after someone hit him."

Jack frowned. "You said four. Alec, was it?"

PJ noted that Jack had a good memory. He may as well get it all out. "What do you know about the Kingdom Mountain theme parks?"

Jack's frown deepened as he thought. "I've heard about them. We had one near us, but it was shut down recently. Wasn't it an orphanage fronting as a theme park?"

PJ nodded, relieved he didn't have to explain. It was hard to talk about that house of horrors. "Lyle, Vinny, and Matt come from the Kingdom Mountain theme park further up the mountain."

"And Aaron?"

"He had his own family from hell, but not from the theme park."

Jack looked away. "You seem to collect boys in need."

"They kind of found us too," PJ said. "They're good boys."

"I'm not like them."

"You're not a boy?" PJ experienced a crushing disappointment he hadn't expected. Unlike his brothers, he wasn't looking for a boy of his own. But this sweet guy, he deserved to belong to a Daddy.

There was a heartbeat of hesitation, then Jack said, "I'm gay, but I'm not a boy."

"Well, that's okay," PJ said with a cheerfulness he didn't feel. "You're welcome here, Jack."

"Thanks." Jack's belly rumbled and he blushed.

PJ grinned at him. "I guess you're hungry. When was the last time you ate?"

"I can't remember."

There were deflections and there were outright lies, and this was a lie, because PJ could clearly see Jack knew when he'd last eaten. And it hadn't been today, or the previous day, judging by his expression. What was it about bringing half-starved boys into their home? Lyle and Vinny had lived on one bowl of oatmeal per day and Aaron barely remembered to eat.

PJ thought about the hungry expression on Jack's face when he'd watched PJ eating pancakes. PJ wasn't much of a cook, but he could make a stack of pancakes and bacon. He went to the pantry and brought out eggs and flour.

It didn't take long before he slid a plate in front of Jack who jolted. PJ hadn't missed that Jack had dozed off. "Wake up, boy."

Jack made a kind of a squeak when he focused on the plate. "This is for me?"

PJ handed him a knife and fork. "All for you. Eat what you can."

He also knew from the boys that it took a while to be able to eat three meals a day when they'd been half-starved. Gruff still had tussles with Lyle over his eating habits. Life lessons didn't change just because he was loved and cared for.

PJ sat with him while Jack ate, telling him tales about his brothers. Most of them were true.

Jack's eyes grew wider and wider as the tales grew more outrageous until finally he burst out, "You're making this up," as PJ told him a story of Harry, an out of control horse, and the delivery man.

"I'm not," PJ protested. "The horse chased the guy into the trees. Harry had to calm the horse and then climb up the tree to rescue the man."

Jack shook his head. "You had a more interesting childhood than I did."

"Where did you live?"

"I don't want to talk about it," Jack said, refusing to meet PJ's gaze.

PJ squeezed his forearm. "You don't have to talk about anything you don't want to."

"Thanks." Jack smiled at him gratefully, then the smile morphed into a yawn.

"I guess you haven't had much sleep recently, huh?"

"No," Jack admitted. "I was afraid I'd end up in the middle of nowhere if I fell asleep."

"You pretty much did, kid. You can take a nap." PJ got to his feet. "You can use Vinny's old room."

He guided Jack out of the kitchen and up the stairs. "Listen, the room is small, but the bed is comfortable. I don't feel right asking you to sleep in my brothers' rooms."

"I'll sleep anywhere," Jack said, and he sounded as if he were about to fall asleep standing up.

PJ guided him into the small bedroom by Damien's room. It had once been a storage closet, until Vinny insisted he needed to sleep near Damien, because Damien was the only one who could calm Vinny's nightmares. Everyone except his big brother knew what Vinny's real agenda was. And finally Vinny got what he wanted, which was a permanent invitation into Damien's bed.

PJ pushed open the door to the bedroom. "Come down when you're ready, Jack. I'll be working in the kitchen for the rest of the afternoon."

Jack slumped wearily on the bed. "Thanks, PJ."

"You're welcome."

PJ left him alone and jogged down the stairs. He had a phone call to make.

"Pablo? It's PJ Brenner."

"Hi, PJ." Pablo sounded distracted. "What can I do for you?"

"I know you filled Aaron's position, but do you have any openings for a bartender?"

Pablo huffed in his ear. "I had to let that guy go. He was always late for his shifts."

"You mean you have a vacancy?" PJ asked.

"I just said that, didn't I? Why? Are you thinking of a career change?"

PJ rolled his eyes at Pablo's belly laugh. "No, but I've got a...friend who needs a job. I don't know if he's got any experience, but I could bring him down tomorrow to talk to you."

"Sure. No promises though. Ten o'clock. Don't be late."

Pablo disconnected the call, leaving PJ grinning at the phone. One thing off the list. Now he just had to help Jack find a home.

"Why are you grinning like an idiot," Brad said as he walked into the kitchen.

"Pablo needs a bartender."

PJ wrinkled his nose at the acrid smell of chemicals clinging to Brad. He had to get over his need to blow things up.

"I thought he'd filled Aaron's post," Brad said, flopping down into his usual seat with a relieved sigh.

"Didn't work out."

"And is this something to do with the cute kid in Vinny's old room?"

PJ scowled at the thought of his brother anywhere near his boy without PJ being there. "You went in?"

"I heard someone snoring. Of course I went in." Brad leaned back in his chair. "So you've got yourself a boy?"

PJ shook his head. "He's not a boy."

Brad looked genuinely confused. "So why is he here?"

"I knocked him out."

Of all the brothers, Brad was the most laid-back and taciturn. It wasn't often anyone surprised him. This time he blinked. "Our boys normally manage that by themselves. Why are you attacking innocent kids?"

"It was an accident, I swear," PJ protested loudly. "I met him in the diner. But he had nowhere to go and no money, so I had to bring him home."

"And you hit him?"

"Yeah." Did Brad keep having to remind him of that?

"But he's not a boy."

Again, they'd been through this.

"No," PJ said shortly.

"So why did he ask if you were his Daddy?"

PJ stared at him. "How did you know?"

Brad tapped his nose, and his smirk grew wide. "I have my sources."

JACK

Terror grabbed Jack by the throat. He stared at the screen.

> I'm going to find you

New message.

> You can't hide from me forever

Jack closed his eyes. There was no way anyone would find him. He'd been so careful to cover his tracks. That's why he had no money.

The door opening nearly made him shed his skin.

PJ beamed at him. "Hey, you're awake."

Jack slipped his phone into his pocket. "Hi, PJ. What time is it?"

He'd had his phone in his hand, but he'd seen nothing but the angry intent of the message.

"It's eight o'clock," PJ said. "I thought you should have dinner and I've got good news."

Dinner sounded good. PJ obviously thought the news was good too, because the big man was positively vibrating.

"Brad wants to meet you and Harry wants to check you're okay. He's a bit of a mother hen."

Jack forced a smile. "I'd like that."

He wanted to beg PJ to stand between him and the rest of the world forever, but he couldn't put PJ and his family in danger. PJ had already been so kind to him. Even bowling him over had been a kindness. He couldn't have stayed in the diner much longer without it being suspicious.

PJ held out his hand. "Jack, whatever's worrying you, my family are good at taking care of people."

Jack gave him a tight smile. He ignored PJ's hand even though he longed just to beg PJ to hold him like he had in the diner. "You're a good man, PJ, but this is my problem. You've already fed me and given me a bed for the night."

PJ's smile vanished and he dropped his hand. "That's the least I could do after assaulting you in the diner. Let's go downstairs or Harry will start fretting about his steaks."

Jack's mouth watered just at the mention of steak. He followed PJ down the stairs and back into the kitchen. Another huge man was there, leaning against the kitchen cabinet while he talked to Harry.

He eyed Jack curiously. "This must be your—"

Harry clapped a hand over his mouth. "Hush."

PJ huffed out a breath. "Jack, this is my really annoying older brother, Brad. You can ignore everything he says."

"Jeez, you're all so big." Jack clapped a hand over his own mouth as they all stared at him. "I'm sorry. I'm not. Big, I mean."

PJ laughed heartily. "It's okay. We won't be offended."

"Good to meet you," Brad said. He didn't offer to shake hands which Jack found kind of odd.

"I thought you'd gotten lost," Harry snapped as he plated up steak and baked potatoes.

Jack couldn't remember the last time he'd been allowed steak. They didn't have money for extravagancies like this. He sat where PJ pointed, and Harry placed a loaded plate in front of him.

"This is for me?"

It was as if he'd flicked a switch. The three men looked at him warily.

PJ turned to him. "You weren't allowed food like this?"

His answer seemed to matter to them. Bizarre.

"We couldn't afford anything like this," Jack said honestly. "Why do you all look so weird?"

PJ seemed to relax. "Eat your food before it gets cold. We'll explain as we eat."

By the time PJ, with Brad's and Harry's interjections, had finished the story of how Lyle and Vinny had lived and Lyle's disbelieving reaction to being allowed food like steak, Jack was halfway through his own meal and staring at them wide-eyed.

"You're not joking."

"I wish we were," Brad growled.

Harry huffed. "I know it sounds fantastical, but every-thing we've told you...it's a thousand times worse in real life."

Jack stared down at his plate. Life had been hard for

him but nothing like that. "They were lucky to find you guys."

"Yeah, they were," PJ agreed. "But my brothers were lucky to find them too."

"Are you guys going to save all your boys?" Jack teased. "Seven saviors for seven boys."

"Seven boys for seven brothers sounds good to me," PJ agreed, his eyes fixed on Jack. "I've got something to tell you. I've found you a job." PJ beamed at him.

Jack blinked, not sure he'd heard him right. "You've found me a job? Where?"

"In the Tin Bar. It's the only gay bar in the town. There's a job for a bartender. You've got an interview first thing tomorrow morning."

"You got me an interview at a bar?" He had to stop echoing PJ's words.

"Yeah. Pablo is a good guy." Then he grimaced. "As long as you don't throw the customers out."

"Why do I feel there's a story about you guys there?" Jack asked.

"Because you know what we're like already," Brad suggested. "It used to be Aaron's job, but he threw us out because of Jake and Pablo didn't like him doing that to his best customers."

Jack furrowed his brow. "Isn't Aaron with Jake?"

"It's a long story." Harry groaned. "But Aaron lost his job and Pablo hasn't found anyone to replace him."

PJ smiled at Jack. "You can tick getting a job off your list."

"I've got to get the job first," Jack pointed out, feeling nervous already.

"You'll be fine," PJ said.

His reassurance made Jack feel better, although he

couldn't trust PJ. Not yet. Despite how kind he'd been to Jack. PJ might throw him out when he found out what Jack had done.

———

The drive down the mountain road the next morning seemed to take forever. Jack tried not to let his nerves get the better of him. He listened to PJ's chatter about the Christmas Tree Farm and living on the mountain. He didn't really listen, but it helped to take his mind off the upcoming interview.

The Tin Bar was an unprepossessing square brick building in a back street. From the outside there was no indication it was a gay bar.

"Are you sure we're in the right place?" Jack muttered as he stood outside the door. His knees nearly buckled when PJ wrapped a meaty arm around his shoulders.

"We're here."

He pushed Jack through the door. The bar was all dark wood and tin tiles on the ceiling, but at least it didn't have moose heads on the walls.

PJ strode over to the bar. "Hi Pablo, I've brought Jack for the interview."

Pablo, a middle-aged balding guy with too-white teeth, studied Jack before he held out his hand. "Jack what?"

Jack gritted his teeth as he took Pablo's hand. He could lie but it was on his ID. "Jack Large."

"Your name is Large?" PJ said in a strangled voice.

Jack didn't even have to look at PJ to know he was trying not to laugh, and Pablo couldn't hide the smirk. "Yeah, yeah."

"Sorry, kid," Pablo said. "But you're standing next to the sasquatch."

One day they'd quit calling him kid, but he'd never grow any taller.

"I can still do the job," Jack insisted.

"Show me your ID," Pablo said.

Jack held out his driver's license and Pablo took it, then looked up at him.

"Huh, you don't look twenty-two."

"I know I look twelve but I'm not."

"A day's trial," Pablo said. "It's Daddies and boys night today. If you can handle that, you've got the job."

"Done." PJ sounded happy.

PJ must be anxious to get rid of him, Jack thought sadly.

"Aaron's room is still vacant," Pablo said. "If you need somewhere to live."

"Jack stays with me until we know this is gonna work out," PJ interrupted before Jack could speak. "We'll be down tonight. I'll take him home at the end of his shift."

Jack turned to look at PJ, but the man was focused on Pablo.

The bar owner glanced at Jack and then back at PJ. "Understood. But you'd better make it clear to the others."

Make what clear? Jack was confused. Then PJ clapped a hand on his shoulder, and he jumped.

"I'll see you later, Jack." He jogged out of the bar and Jack felt he could breathe again. PJ dominated the room.

Pablo looked at Jack. "What do you know about bartending?"

"Nothing," Jack said, "but I can learn."

Pablo sighed. "You can't be worse than the last guy. Grab that tray and collect the glasses from the tables. You've got a long day ahead of you."

Jack hadn't worked so hard in his life. His shoulders and arms ached from lifting barrels and his feet ached from being on them all day. But he hadn't had time to think or brood, which was a good thing. No messages on his phone was even better.

Daddies and boys night was about to start. He was curious to see what would happen. He also knew he'd see PJ again which made his stomach flutter.

The Daddies swept in, holding the hands of their boys. He knew from Pablo it wasn't a big group, and usually dominated by PJ and his brothers. But it gave the littles a chance to play and the Daddies to talk together. And it was just like that. The littles rushed off to play with the cars and trains, and the Daddies gathered in a corner. They looked at him curiously but beyond that, no one paid him much attention.

Jack knew the minute the three Brenner boys swept into the bar. The atmosphere grew charged. The unattached boys started fluttering, even those with Daddies looking their way, and the Daddies started to scowl. It would only take one thing to light the touchpaper.

PJ grinned at him as he reached the bar. "How's it going?"

"Good," Jack said.

PJ leaned on the bar, his blue eyes twinkling as he grinned. Jack noticed the fan of lines that deepened around PJ's eyes when he laughed. He wondered how old PJ was.

"I bet your feet hurt."

"Like crazy," Jack confessed.

PJ let out a rumbling belly laugh. "You'll get used to it. See you later."

Brad and Harry waved at Jack who smiled at them. He knew it was going to be hard as hell to focus with PJ in the bar.

PJ and that twink who sat on his lap and licked him up like he was cotton candy.

Watching that did not help his concentration and after Jack got the order wrong twice, Pablo sent him to pick up the empty glasses. Jack growled under his breath as he collected the glasses on the tray. He cleared a small round table. He turned and sent the tray and glasses flying as someone swept Jack into his arms.

"Found you," the man hissed.

3

PJ

The moment PJ heard breaking glass he knew Jack was in trouble. He swung around to see Jack struggling to free himself from the arms of one of the town Daddies.

Flames exploded in PJ's head. No one hurt his boy! He pushed the twink off his lap and leapt to his feet, ignoring the confused "What's up, bro?" from Brad.

"I've found my boy for the night," the beefy man said, wearing a huge grin. He was at least a foot shorter than PJ, but solidly built. They were friends, kind of, but not when the man was scaring PJ's boy.

"Put my boy down, Travis," PJ bellowed.

Earl Travis looked over his shoulder and glowered at PJ. "Hands off, Brenner. This one's mine. You've got your own."

He was a good Daddy, popular with the boys, but something had gotten into him tonight. He would never usually just grab a boy without consent.

PJ stalked toward the two men. "I think you'll find he's under my protection. Let him go."

But Travis didn't budge an inch as he ignored Jack's struggles.

"What the hell's going on here," Pablo yelled from behind the bar.

"Nothing," Jack said, his voice shaky. "Nothing at all. It was a misunderstanding, wasn't it?"

He looked pleadingly at PJ who gave a curt nod. PJ knew Jack was trying to defuse the situation, but Jack was still clutched in Travis's arms.

"Let go of me before PJ tears you limb from limb," Jack hissed at Travis.

PJ thought his boy had a remarkably sound grasp of the situation.

Pablo stalked toward them. "Let my boy go."

PJ turned on him. *My boy!*

But Pablo fixed him with a glare. "Sit down, PJ."

PJ stayed where he was. He took a step toward Travis who had the sense to let go of Jack, who wriggled away. PJ was about to sweep Jack into his arms when Pablo spoke.

"Travis, touch my staff again and you're barred. Jack, sweep up the mess."

PJ thought that was unfair as Jack hadn't been responsible for the mess, but he received another pleading look from Jack.

Travis muttered an apology at Jack and vanished back to his table. PJ sat down with his brothers, but he didn't take his gaze off Jack as he retrieved the tray and swept up the shards of glass. He watched Jack anxiously as Pablo talked to him. It wouldn't be fair if he lost his job because of an over-excited Daddy.

"You should have told me you were taken," the twink

said reproachfully.

PJ looked at him. "I'm not. Jack isn't a boy, but he's under my protection until he's settled."

The twink rolled his eyes. "You can't be that blind."

PJ scowled and the twink hastily apologized.

"I'm sorry, PJ, but he's your boy whether he knows it or not."

PJ gazed at Jack and sighed. "I wish he were mine. Then I'd kill anyone who touched him."

The twink patted his shoulder. "You show him what a great Daddy you can be."

He bounced away and headed straight for Travis, sitting in his lap with a triumphant toss of his head at PJ. Travis went from dejected to beaming, his arms around the twink.

Brad raised an eyebrow at PJ. "You gonna take over Jake's role while he's away?"

PJ couldn't pretend to know what he meant. "I *am* an ass. And Jack needs my help."

"He needs a Daddy," Harry muttered.

"He says he's not a boy."

"And you believe him?"

PJ looked at Jack who was now back behind the bar. Jack caught his gaze and gave him a small smile. PJ gave him a reassuring smile in return. "I don't know what to believe."

"Who are you and what did you do with my ass of a brother?" At PJ's scowl, Brad just rolled his eyes. "Why do my brothers turn into idiots when they meet their boy? What would you do to any other boy? Go all Daddy on his butt."

"That's your advice, is it?" PJ asked.

"It works for me."

As PJ couldn't remember the last time Brad had gone

Daddy on anyone, he doubted that, but he knew Brad only had his best interests at heart. But being PJ, he had to push back. "When are you going to go Daddy on any boy's ass."

"When I find him," Brad said easily, ignoring PJ's challenge. "Look at you guys. Five down, me and Harry to go."

Alec and Matt weren't officially a couple but PJ knew it was only a matter of time. Could it be that easy? PJ glanced at Jack again.

"I want him to trust me," he murmured.

"Then let him know you're there for him, body and soul."

PJ gave Brad the side-eye. "You're not gonna write poetry about this, are you?"

"Unless I can set you on fire, probably not," Brad assured him.

"Why did I have to get stuck with the weird brothers?" Harry complained at random.

PJ loved his brothers, but dear God, they were annoying. He got up and sauntered to the bar.

"What can I get you?" Jack asked.

He leaned on the bar. "Three bottles of water, please."

Jack fetched him the bottles from the refrigerator and filled glasses with ice.

"Are you okay?" PJ said, so quietly no one else could hear him.

"I am now. I thought Pablo might fire me for the broken glasses, but he said that wasn't my fault." Jack leaned forward. "And he's gonna be having a word with that Daddy too."

PJ breathed easier. After Pablo's overreaction with Aaron and what could have happened if Jake hadn't found Aaron lying on the side of the road, PJ wasn't leaving anything to chance.

He smiled at Jack and took the bottles and glasses back to the table.

The evening dragged on. PJ hadn't ever felt it had taken so long before. He gave Brad and Harry space because he realized having publicly claimed Jack, no one was going to go near him now, and he didn't want to cramp their evening. He would usually have sat at the bar, but he didn't want to crowd on Jack. PJ retreated to a small table and watched the littles play together.

He could really have done with Damien or Gruff here, brothers who'd found their boys. Jake and Aaron were still so new, their relationship squeaked around the edges. PJ wasn't used to this uncertainty. He felt a responsibility for Jack. He did knock him out after all. All he wanted was to make sure the boy had a job and somewhere to call home. If Jack wasn't looking for a Daddy, then PJ could make sure Jack had a friend.

A small ball rolled over and nudged his foot. One of the blond littles glanced at him uncertainly. PJ smiled and rolled it back. The little burst into wide smiles and carried on playing with the ball.

"Thank you," a quiet voice said.

PJ looked up to see a silver-haired, older man smiling at him. "No problem."

"May I join you?" He wasn't local for sure. More west coast than east coast. And certainly not one of the local Daddies who wore plaid shirts and Wranglers. This Daddy was older and dressed in an immaculate, dark-charcoal suit and white shirt. His styled hair was almost white. A real handsome silver fox.

"You're welcome." PJ indicated a free seat. He could do with the distraction from thinking about Jack.

"I'm Graham Knight," the silver fox said, "and the boy

you just rolled the ball to is Ian, my little."

PJ offered his hand. "PJ Brenner. Good to meet you, Graham. Is this your first time here?"

"It is. We're passing through."

Kingdom Mountain wasn't really on the way to anywhere, but who was PJ to argue?

"Which little is yours?" Knight's handshake was firm.

"None of them." PJ couldn't help glancing over to Jack.

Knight followed his gaze. "Ah, now I understand the confrontation."

"He's not mine either. Jack is a friend. I'm helping him at the moment, and I don't want anyone taking advantage of him."

"I'm sure the boy appreciates it."

PJ bristled at the condescending 'the boy'. "He's not a boy."

Knight gifted him with the same 'You've got to be kidding me' look Brad had.

"He says he's not a boy." PJ shrugged. "I'm not going to pressure him, but I'm gonna take care of him as long as he needs me. And that includes making sure he's not harassed by other Daddies."

Knight inclined his head and PJ got the feeling he'd received Knight's approval. "That makes you a good Daddy."

PJ looked at Jack again who was now serving a small boy. "I hope he'll understand that." Then he studied Knight. "You're a long way from home. What are you really doing here?"

Knight gave him a thin smile. "Things got difficult at home. Ian insisted we took a break. It's a hard thing for an old man to realize it's time he moved on. Let younger blood take over."

PJ heard the pain in his voice. "I'm sorry."

He saw Ian look up, narrow his eyes, then he crawled over and into Knight's lap. He chattered away to his Daddy about one of the toys and Knight gave him a tender smile. Knight knew as well as PJ did that Ian was trying to comfort him.

Knight sighed as Ian settled against him. "I recognize your surname. I think we might have a mutual acquaintance."

"Oh?" PJ couldn't think of anyone like Knight.

"Quinn Ryder."

It took a moment for PJ to place the name, then he remembered the huge man in black leathers who'd come to the cabin occasionally. "I know him, although my brothers know him better."

"Ian is in a band with his boy."

PJ looked at Ian with dawning respect. "You're in Daysance?"

"I am," the little said shyly.

"Quinn's boy is Cade Connolly," Knight said.

PJ shook his head in disbelief. He was just a guy who lived on a mountain. He looked at Jack again. Would Jack be content with a simple Daddy like him?

JACK

Jack gritted his teeth as PJ talked to the older Daddy in the sharp suit for most of the evening. The fact that PJ had ignored him since the issue with Travis rankled. At least Harry and Brad had checked on him even though they'd been occupied with cute guys. It was sweet to watch how gentle and kind these huge men were with the twinks on their laps, and how many boys cast longing looks their way.

But after rescuing him from Earl Travis's attention, PJ hadn't come near him.

Jack kept reminding himself this was his trial day for a new job. He couldn't afford to screw it up. If he got a job, he could find somewhere to live, and only then could he think about his greatest desire. Finding a Daddy of his own.

Except, he'd found the Daddy he wanted. Right over there, watching the littles. Jack had nearly stomped over and yelled "My Daddy!" when one of them rolled a ball to PJ to get his attention.

Thank goodness he hadn't. It didn't take Jack long to realize the scruffy blond little belonged to the silver fox. And by the way the boy rushed to comfort him when his Daddy looked distressed, it was a deep emotional bond.

"Jack!"

Jack turned to see his boss scowling at him. "I'm sorry, Pablo. I was...uh...distracted."

Pablo rolled his eyes. "Listen, kid, you've done well. I know it's been a long day but keep your head in the game until we close in an hour, and you've got yourself a job."

"Really?" God, the relief was overwhelming. He'd gotten himself a job...if he made it to the end of the shift.

Jack took a deep breath and forced himself to focus on the work. He even managed to be calm and polite when he collected glasses from PJ's table.

PJ gave him an anxious smile when he came over. "Is everything okay? I saw Pablo talking to you."

So maybe PJ hadn't been completely ignoring him. Jack smiled at him. "If I don't screw up between now and the end of the shift, I've got the job!"

PJ broke into the widest smile he'd seen and got up to hug him tightly.

"Oof!" Jack gasped. "Let me go, you big oaf, before I get

fired."

"Sorry." PJ let him go but his smile was still huge. "Well done, boy! I mean, Jack. Well done! And you haven't thrown anyone out."

Jack snorted. "There's still time." He grinned as he headed to the other tables. He heard the silver Daddy say, "It sounds like a story there."

Jack went around the tables, collecting glasses, and made an effort to talk to everyone. If he was going to work here, he ought to get to know their names. But after the third time the Daddy sent an anxious look in PJ's direction before he responded, Jack gave up. He got it. PJ had claimed him even if he was only protecting Jack. There was now an invisible bubble around Jack, and no one was going to talk to him or lay a finger on him without PJ's permission. Jack didn't know whether to feel flattered or annoyed.

What Jack was, he decided at the end of his shift, was exhausted. Weary to his bones. And his feet ached like hell. He'd had breaks and Pablo had taken him to the diner during the day, with a growled "Don't expect this every day, kid." He was grateful PJ had stayed to drive him back, because all Jack wanted to do was fall into bed.

Brad and Harry had vanished an hour earlier with a "See you at home," from Harry, and two disappointed boys.

Pablo handed him an envelope. "There's your pay. Be here tomorrow at three."

Jack's mouth dropped open. "Pay?"

"Don't question it," PJ hissed in a stage whisper. "Or he'll take it back."

"You're an ass, Brenner," Pablo growled.

PJ threw his arms out, almost felling Jack again. "Is that the way to speak to the man who found you a new bartender?"

"If you knock me out again, I won't be able to work," Jack grumbled.

"Yeah, be careful," Pablo mocked.

PJ huffed, but his grin was huge, and the laughter lines crinkled around his eyes. It was really sexy. Jack had to move this along before he popped a boner in front of his new boss.

As they walked to the parking lot, he said, "PJ, will you be able to drive me tomorrow afternoon?" To his relief, PJ nodded.

"I've got to come into town with logs, but in future you could borrow our old pickup. It's Jake's but he won't care. It's not like he needs it now. Have you got a driver's license?"

Jack blinked. Didn't every kid learn to drive? Then he thought of the boys in the Brenner household. Maybe not. "I can drive."

"Great. The pickup is old, but she goes just fine."

"Are you sure Jake won't mind?" Jack asked.

"I'll call him," PJ said. "But most of us use the pickup when we need to. I don't want to take the truck every time. If Jake's on a case, they take Alec's Chevy. It looks more professional."

"If I find a room in town, I won't need it." Jack glanced at PJ when there was no immediate response and caught his tight-lipped expression. "PJ, what's wrong?"

"Nothing."

Nothing was the equivalent of fine. A blatant lie if ever there was one, but Jack didn't feel he could push it. He got into the pickup when PJ unlocked it.

PJ drove out of the parking lot and onto the highway, heading for the mountain road.

Jack sought for something to say to break the uncomfortable silence between them. "Who was the silver fox? He didn't dress like the rest of you."

"He's from out of town. It turns out we have a mutual friend who's working with Jake and Alec."

"He looked a bit overdressed," Jack teased.

PJ chuckled. "Yeah, I think he was expecting more than a small town bar. His boy is in a band. Daysance."

Jack choked. "Really?"

"You know them?"

Of course Jack knew Daysance. He'd have to have his head stuck under a rock not to have heard of their phenomenal success. He was into heavier rock than their pop, but they were good, especially with Cade Connolly at the lead.

"I'm not into pop," PJ confessed. "I prefer country."

"I don't mind country. My gran listened to the radio all the time so I've got a wide taste." PJ made a strange noise in the back of his throat and Jack turned to him. "What?"

"Boys, well, everyone, laughs at me for liking country. You can imagine what it was like in a family with six brothers who love heavy rock."

"You should put them over your knee and spank their ass for being rude to you," Jack declared, his voice more heated than he'd intended. He didn't like the idea of anyone being rude to his Daddy.

"Maybe I should."

Jack couldn't see PJ's expression. They'd left the lights of the town far behind them. But PJ sounded pleased at Jack defending him. "PJ?"

PJ glanced at him. "Yeah?"

"How old are you?"

"I'm thirty-five. The middle brother."

After that, conversation died, and Jack wasn't surprised

when a change in noise woke him, and he realized they'd reached the cabin.

"I'm sorry." He yawned. "I didn't mean to fall asleep."

"No problem," PJ said. "You've had a long day. Let's eat and you can go to bed. Pablo will work you just as hard tomorrow."

"You made me dinner?"

"Of course," PJ said, like it was a strange question. "You've got to eat."

Jack wasn't sure he could stay awake long enough to eat, but he was also sure PJ wouldn't let him go to bed without some food in his belly.

He shuffled into the cabin, took off his jacket, and sat down to unlace his boots.

"Come into the kitchen when you're ready," PJ said.

Jack grunted and followed PJ into the kitchen. From the sweet smell, there was a pan of hot chocolate on the stove-top. PJ followed his gaze and within a minute he had a large cup of chocolaty goodness in his hands. He sipped it and almost moaned as the smooth flavor slipped down his throat. It tasted so good.

"Did you make this?" he asked.

PJ nodded. "I drink most of it, so I get to make it. At least that's what Harry and Brad keep telling me. It's not as good as Lyle's."

"It tastes just fine to me," Jack assured him.

Jack sat down at the table. His nose ran and he reached into his jeans pocket for a tissue, only to hear something fall onto the floor.

In horror, Jack watched his yellow Binky roll under the kitchen table. He looked up to see PJ's attention fixed on the pacifier.

"It's not mine," he said quickly.

4

PJ

PJ folded his beefy arms across his wide chest and pinned Jack to the spot with his glower. He noticed the way Jack's eyes roamed over him and the boy swallowed hard. Point made.

He raised an eyebrow. "Oh? Not yours? You were just carrying it for a friend?"

"I..." Jack trailed off, not sure what to say.

"Maybe you found it at the club?"

Jack didn't respond. He just stared miserably at the pacifier.

PJ retrieved the Binky, ran it under the faucet, and returned it to Jack, who clutched it as if it were a lifeline.

"This is yours, isn't it?" PJ said, letting his voice soften.

Jack nodded.

"And you're a boy, aren't you?" PJ demanded.

Jack nodded again.

"You lied to me." PJ was hurt but not surprised. It wasn't as if he hadn't guessed the secret Jack was hiding.

Another miserable nod. Jack refused to look at him.

"You didn't want to tell me?"

"No."

"No what."

"No, Daddy," Jack whispered, scuffing the tiles with his toes.

At that moment Brad walked into the kitchen, looked at PJ, then at Jack. Obviously sensing the tension, he walked back out and shut the kitchen door. PJ would thank him later.

"Why didn't you want me to know?"

"I didn't *know* you," Jack burst out. "Men call themselves Daddies, but they're not, not really. You said you were seven gay Daddies. I..."

PJ waited but Jack didn't finish his sentence. "You didn't believe me?"

Jack nodded. "You can't all be Daddies."

PJ thought about his brothers. Seven huge bears of men who each wanted nothing more than to have a boy of his own to take care of. "You're right."

Jack's head shot up. "I am?"

"You don't know me or my brothers." Yes, PJ was hurt, but he understood Jack's reasoning. "But we're all Daddies."

PJ took Jack's cup, topped off the hot chocolate for something to do, then filled two more cups.

"Take these to Brad and Harry. They'll be in the den. Come back here."

Jack jumped up to obey. He picked up the cups and PJ opened the door. He pointed toward the den, and left Jack to it. PJ filled a final cup and sat down at the table. He took a long swallow, needing the sugar to focus.

Jack returned, shut the kitchen door, and took his seat again, his head bowed. "They both said thank you."

PJ pulled out his phone and scrolled through his photos, pressing one.

"This is the seven of us five years ago." He turned his phone to show Jack.

Jack studied the photo carefully. "You look so young there."

PJ smiled ruefully. "We were. Gruff was barely older than you."

It was before Lyle, before evil CEOs, before their innocent world was turned upside down.

He scrolled to the next picture. "And this is us with our boys."

Seven Daddies, with their boys. Some older, some littles, a princess. All treated like they were special for the night. It had been one hell of a night. He smiled as he looked at the boy on his knees. Stevie had been high maintenance, but one heck of a boy. PJ had learned a lot from him.

Jack blinked at the picture. "You all had boys?"

"This is the one time we all had boys back for the night. It was Gruff's birthday. We celebrated at home. They all knew us and trusted us to come back here. We made sure they all knew they were safe. You can meet one or two still at the Tin Bar."

Not Stevie though. He would never introduce Jack to Stevie. Jack would go running.

"Not the boys in your family now."

PJ shook his head and scrolled through his phone. "This is Lyle not long after Gruff found him." Lyle had that shell-shocked expression that took months to fade. "This is him now." Lyle was on Gruff's lap, curled into his strong body, smiling up at him.

Jack reached out a finger, as if he were going to touch Lyle, then pulled back. "He looks so happy."

"That's because he is. And this is Vinny. He claimed Damien the moment he met him." PJ watched his oldest grumpy brother fall in love without even knowing it.

"He's very young," Jack observed.

"Legal and was never going to let anyone come between him and Damien."

One more scroll. "This is Aaron. The bruising is from a truck driver who took exception to Aaron liking guys. And this is Aaron with Jake, just before they left for the road trip."

"Why are you showing me all these?" Jack asked.

"Because I can't think of any other way of showing you that we are who we say we are. We grow Christmas trees and are Daddies."

Jack chewed on his bottom lip. "Do you share?"

PJ choked on his drink, the hot chocolate spraying over the table. Jack jumped back, out of reach.

"What the hell?" PJ gasped.

He grabbed a cloth from the sink and wiped his face and then the table before the mess spread.

Jack's face tightened. "It's a fair question."

PJ supposed it was and Jack was owed an honest answer. "I've never shared a boy. I'm a one-boy Daddy. When I was younger, I had the odd threesome. I like my kink. But not with boys. They deserve my whole attention."

"Thanks." Jack looked anywhere but at PJ. "I needed to know."

PJ sat down again. "Jack, I need you to answer a question for me. Did a Daddy try to share you?"

Jack shook his head. "I was lucky. Someone warned me off before I got involved."

PJ breathed easier. "You carry a Binky. So you're a little? How old are you."

"I don't really know. Maybe three or four. I've never had time to explore. This—" Jack opened his fingers to show the faded yellow pacifier. "—was mine when I was a baby. It's like a comfort blanket."

"I understand. It's precious to you." PJ furrowed his brow. "I haven't seen you use it here."

"No," Jack murmured.

PJ understood. Jack had used his pacifier in private. He was learning that what Jack *didn't* say was as important as what he did. "Jack, I don't want to put pressure on you. As I said before, I want to help you."

"You've already found me a job. You don't have to do anything else."

"And I'll help you find somewhere to live too. You're under my protection now."

Jack stared at him, and PJ knew he was trying to work out if PJ was full of shit or not. PJ knew for the first time in his life he had to convince another human he could be a responsible Daddy. PJ was an ass. Hell, he loved being an ass. But Jack needed someone who could take care of him.

"You don't have to do this. I can—"

"It's non-negotiable," PJ said firmly. He got to his feet. "More hot chocolate?"

Jack gave a jaw-cracking yawn. "I should go to bed."

"What about dinner? You should eat."

"I'm not hungry," Jack admitted. "I need sleep more than food."

PJ wondered if he should press the issue. His brothers

were always insisting their boys ate, but Jack looked dead on his feet, and he had worked all day.

"Go to bed," he said.

Jack got wearily to his feet. "Thanks for taking care of me, PJ. I don't know what I'd have done without you."

"You'd have managed. I have faith in you."

Jack gave him a tired smile and headed to the door. PJ wanted to go with him. To put him to bed. But Jack still hadn't accepted PJ as his Daddy.

PJ stayed where he was as he heard Jack walk up the stairs. He wasn't surprised when Harry and Brad walked in, cups in hand, and headed for the stovetop.

"Where's your boy?" Harry demanded as he refilled his cup.

"Gone to bed," PJ said shortly, "and he's not my boy."

"Without you?" Brad looked astonished. "What are you sitting there for? Go after him."

"He's not my boy," PJ repeated.

"It didn't look like that when I came in earlier. You were all Daddy then. I thought Jack's eyes were gonna pop, they were so wide."

Yeah, that had been satisfying, but PJ had to be honest. "I was *a* Daddy. Just not *his* Daddy."

"I'll go put him to bed," Harry said, turning to the door.

"No!" PJ sprang to his feet, the chair tipping over with a clatter. He would tackle Harry if necessary. Then he caught the smug expression on Harry's and Brad's faces and growled at them.

"So not *your* boy, but he can't be anyone else's," Harry said.

"Fuck off," PJ muttered. Sometimes it was worth a dollar. He would really have to apologize to Damien for all the times PJ had teased him about Vinny.

"He's left his Binky," Brad said.

PJ stared at the pacifier on the table. It hadn't been there before Jack left the room. He was sure of it.

"What more do you need, little brother?"

"I—"

Harry slung an arm around PJ's shoulders. "He left it there because he doesn't have the words to ask for you. The question is, what are you going to do about it?"

JACK

Jack sat on the bed and waited but PJ didn't follow him.

He waited some more. Then he huffed because he was sure PJ would follow him. PJ wanted to be his Daddy, didn't he?

He wanted his Binky back. He put his hand in his pocket, but it wasn't there. He could go downstairs and get it, but he'd thought...hoped...PJ would bring it up with him.

Jack snuggled into a fetal position, and sucked his thumb, trying to comfort himself. He wanted his Binky. He wanted his Daddy.

He wrapped himself around one of the pillows and closed his eyes, knowing he was exhausted, and he'd have a long day ahead of him tomorrow. Maybe he could take a short nap and go downstairs to retrieve it when the brothers were asleep.

———

Jack didn't know if he was dreaming or not, but he felt someone caress his hair and he was sure he felt a soft kiss on his cheek.

"Kisses, Daddy."

He swore there was another kiss on his cheek.

"Jack? Wake up, little one. You'll be more comfortable if you were undressed."

Jake opened his eyes and blinked sleepily at PJ who knelt beside him. "My Binky?

"I've got it, boy."

PJ pressed it into Jack's hand. Jack popped it into his mouth and sucked hard.

"Let's get you into bed," PJ said. "Take out your pacifier for a moment."

Jack grumbled as PJ coaxed him to sit up, but he raised his arms as PJ tugged off his hoody.

"Do you wear pajamas?" he asked.

Jack flushed, but he pulled out his onesie from under the pillow. It was decorated with rockets and stars and moons.

"Good boy," PJ murmured.

Jack let PJ strip him and redress him in the onesie, then he snuggled under the covers. PJ nudged the Binky against his lips and Jack sucked it into his mouth. He sighed happily and closed his eyes. He felt the lightest of kisses to his cheek.

"Good night, my boy, sleep well," PJ murmured.

"G'nite, Daddy," Jake said and was asleep before PJ left the room.

———

Jack nearly fell out of bed when someone banged hard on the door.

"Jack, get out of bed. Breakfast is ready."

He wrinkled his brow. That wasn't his Daddy. Where was PJ?

Another thunderous knock. "Jack!"

Jack wrinkled his brow. Was that Brad?

"I'm awake," he croaked, suddenly realizing Brad could come in and see him in his onesie. He pulled the covers up to his chin just in case.

"Finally. Listen, PJ's had to go to town early. I'll drive you to work. But you need to hurry up."

"I'll be downstairs in five minutes."

Jack heard footsteps go downstairs. He sat up and looked for his Binky. Then he realized he was sitting on it. He dug it out, popped it into his mouth, and sucked furiously, trying to clear his head.

PJ was in town. Brad was going to give him a ride to work. Jack needed to shift his ass out of bed. He could do that. He tried not to be hurt that PJ had left without waking him.

He dug into his pack. He was going to have to do laundry soon as he had no clean clothes. Maybe the brothers wouldn't mind if he offered to do some of their laundry too.

Jack heard Brad in the kitchen, talking to Harry. He paused outside the door, not wanting to interrupt their conversation.

"They've closed Dallas and now Kentucky. It looks as if Damien and Vinny will be back sooner than they expected," Harry said.

"They're done with their road trip?" Brad asked.

"So done. Damien said he never wanted to go off the mountain again."

Both brothers chuckled.

Then Brad said, "What about the others?"

"Gruff's trying to persuade Lyle to take a break, but the

boy is proving stubborn. He's wrecked by what he's seen. I told him to go all Daddy Bear on Lyle's ass."

"What did Gruff say?"

"You don't want to know," Harry said, "but he owes five dollars to the jar. I think he needs us."

"We've got to get them home soon," Brad agreed.

Jack could hear the longing in his voice. It seemed all the brothers hated this enforced separation.

"Where's that boy?"

"I'm here." Jack hurried into the kitchen.

"Finally," Brad snapped and thrust a cup of coffee at him.

Jack thought he was lucky not to be wearing the coffee. "What time is it?"

"Eleven-thirty. Pablo called. He needs you in early."

Eleven-thirty? Jack blinked. He couldn't remember the last time he slept in so late.

"Sorry to wake you, kid. I know you weren't due in til later, but Pablo was desperate." Brad grimaced. "He's always like that."

Jack ran his hand through his hair. "It's okay. I need the hours. Thanks for the coffee." He murmured a good morning at Harry, who gave him a lazy wave.

Meanwhile Brad was on a roll. "I made you a sandwich you can eat on the way. Let's go."

He virtually shoved Jack out of the kitchen. Jack felt like a lamb being herded by a giant bear. A bear who smelled of explosives. That wasn't worrying at all.

"What's PJ doing?" he asked.

"He's—" Brad rolled his eyes as PJ's truck screeched to a halt in front of them. "Worrying about you."

Jack couldn't help the warmth that spread through him at the realization PJ had rushed back for him.

"Why isn't Jack at work yet?" PJ snarled at his brother. He steered Jack to the truck. "Come on, we've got to go."

"Thanks for getting my boy up and ready, Brad." Brad grumbled. "Thanks for making his breakfast, Brad."

"Yeah, yeah, sorry. Come on." PJ almost threw Jack into the truck and ran around the hood to the driver's side.

Jack clutched onto his food as they squealed away. "I don't think I'm that late."

PJ grunted. "I don't want to give Pablo a chance to fire you. Eat your breakfast."

"Yes, Daddy." That just slipped out with the order.

Jack unwrapped the paper and nibbled at the bread. He wasn't really hungry. It took him a while to work up to food in the morning. But he didn't want to annoy PJ and it had been kind of Brad to make it for him.

"Have you got your Binky?" PJ demanded.

Jack slipped his hand in his pocket and felt the familiar weight of the pacifier. "I've got it."

"Good. I'm going to be in this evening to collect you. I've told Pablo you can't work another long day."

Jack stiffened as PJ just walked over his life without even asking if that was okay. "Surely that's my decision, not yours."

PJ had been about to drive away, but he turned to Jack, an unusually serious expression on his face. "You're under my protection, Jack, until you're settled. Pablo will work you into the ground if you don't set boundaries. I love the guy, but I know what he's like. You don't. Let me set the boundaries until you're ready to take over."

Jack chewed on his lip. He should be standing on his own feet, not letting PJ run his life. But he wanted to rest his head on PJ's massive chest and let his Daddy make all the decisions for him.

Obviously seeing the conflict in Jack's expression, PJ fixed Jack with a stare. "Boy, you will let me take care of you. Now eat your breakfast."

"Yes, Daddy," Jack whispered.

PJ gave a curt nod and they drove out of the drive and onto the mountain road.

Jack ate the sandwich and drank the coffee. He felt settled, more grounded once he'd eaten the food. He was stupid to argue with PJ. One day into the job and Pablo called him in early. PJ was right. He needed a job with regular hours, not to be worked into the ground.

"Feeling better?" PJ asked, and now his voice was softer.

"I am," Jack admitted. "Thanks."

His phone buzzed but he ignored it. It buzzed again.

"Don't you want to look at that?" PJ asked.

That was the last thing Jack wanted to do, but he knew PJ would push and push until Jack was spilling out his whole toxic story. Then Jack might find himself alone.

He pulled out his phone and looked at the screen.

> You can't hide forever

Jack swallowed hard. He had to leave now. Before someone hurt PJ.

> When I find you, you're dead

5

P J gripped the steering wheel hard, concentrating on the bends in the road. He couldn't stop here but when it was safe, he'd pull over and find out what the heck had frightened Jack so much his hands shook violently.

Jack stared out of the window, not hearing PJ's murmured, "Boy?"

The second they were off the mountain road PJ pulled over and turned to Jack, who blinked at him in surprise.

"PJ, what's wrong?"

PJ clenched his jaw. "You tell me, boy."

"I don't know what you mean. I thought you were taking me to the bar." But Jack refused to meet his gaze.

PJ wished Gruff was here. Or even Damien. They were so much better at dealing with boys who needed careful handling. PJ was a bull when it came to guys. He wanted to throw Jack over his shoulder, take him to bed, and hide him from the world.

But he tried again. "Why are you so scared, little one?"

"I'm not," Jack muttered.

"Then why are your hands shaking?"

Jack clenched his hands into fists so tightly his knuckles were white. "It's nothing."

PJ reached over and took one of Jack's fists in his much larger hand. "You're a terrible liar."

That made Jack laugh, even if it sounded bitter. "Tell me something I don't know."

"Jack, what did the message say?"

"Dammit, PJ, just let it go, okay?"

"You don't trust me?" That was a bitter pill to swallow.

But Jack looked at him for the first time. "I do trust you."

"Then why won't you tell me?"

"Because I don't want you to get hurt. Don't you understand? I need to protect you."

PJ barked out a laugh and Jack tugged his hand back, hurt in his eyes as he thought PJ was mocking him.

"No baby, I'm not laughing at you." PJ took Jack's hand again. "It's just, have you seen me? Who do you think can hurt me?"

But Jack's expression didn't lighten. "You don't know him. He hurts people."

"*Who* hurts people? Who is he?"

"I can't tell you."

"Can't or won't?" PJ pressed.

Silence.

"Is this why you ran away? From that person?"

Jack nodded reluctantly.

"Did he hurt you?" PJ's voice hardened at the thought of his boy being hurt by another man.

Jack shook his head.

"But he threatened to."

"I took something of his. He wants it back."

"What did you take?"

"Beans."

PJ furrowed his brow. He just swore he heard Jack mumble something about beans. He was about to query it when his phone rang. He sighed as he saw the Tin Bar number flash up. "Pablo."

"Where the hell is that boy of yours?" Pablo snapped.

"We're on our way."

"You'd better be or this ain't gonna work."

PJ was tempted to tell Pablo where to shove his job, but he caught Jack's pleading look. "I'm sorry, Pablo. It's my fault. We'll be there in twenty."

He disconnected the call before Pablo shouted at him again. His tolerance would only go so far. Then he looked at Jack. "This isn't finished, boy, but you have to get to work. You and I are going to talk later though. It's my job to protect you and I can't do that if I don't know what to expect."

"You didn't know me two days ago," Jack whispered.

"What's that got to do with it?" PJ asked. "I knew you were mine from the moment I saw you."

"When you knocked me unconscious?"

"No, when I saw you drinking coffee. I knew then I'd go to the ends of the earth to protect you."

Jack stared at him as if he'd grown two heads.

"Too much?" PJ queried. Dammit, he knew he was the wrong person for the job. He'd already scared Jack with his declaration. This was why he'd always been one of those no commitment Daddies.

"No one has ever wanted to take care of me before," Jack whispered.

"Oh."

PJ started the truck before he got himself into more trouble. They were back on the road again before Jack spoke.

"Do you mean it?"

"I do."

"Getting ahead of yourself, aren't you?" Jack said.

"Huh…oh. Cheeky brat." Throwing his own words back in his face. PJ couldn't help a quick smile at Jack and saw it echoed in Jack's smirk.

They were almost at the bar when Jack said, "PJ?"

"Yeah, little one?"

"This isn't gonna work, is it?"

PJ's heart sank as he pulled into the parking lot. "What do you mean, boy?"

"Taking me to work every day. You've got your own work to do. I should find a place in town." Jack didn't sound happy about the idea, but PJ understood he was trying to be helpful.

"I understand you want your independence," PJ said carefully, "but you're new in town and you've only just started working at the bar. How about we give it another couple of days before you think about finding somewhere to live?"

He heard a huff from Jack but when PJ glanced at him, he couldn't miss Jack's relieved expression. PJ patted Jack's thigh. "Don't rush it, Jack. Let me take care of you a bit longer." PJ didn't want to pressure Jack, but he was concerned Jack was trying to run before he could walk. He would take care of Jack for as long as the boy would let him.

"A bit longer," Jack whispered.

"Good boy. Now you need to get inside before Pablo has an aneurysm."

Jack opened the car door, then leaned over to PJ and kissed his cheek. "Thank you," he whispered. "And you need to trim your beard."

PJ huffed and Jack laughed.

Cheeky boy. PJ liked his wild beard. It went with his mountain man persona.

PJ had things he wanted to do in town. He went to the stores to pick up supplies. He wanted to be ready for when his brothers returned home. He also had another place to visit, one that was only known to the Daddies and boys in the local area.

He pushed open the door and the woman looked up from her sewing machine. She appeared to be sewing a pretty blue dress with lace around the bottom.

"Hi, Brenda," PJ said, flashing her his huge smile.

"PJ Brenner. It's been a long time since you came to visit me. I thought you'd forgotten all about me."

Brenda was a short, round woman with a shock of red hair and the brightest green eyes he'd ever seen.

PJ caught her into a hug. "Hey, lovely lady. It's been a long while since I've had a reason to come back."

Brenda gave him a speculative look. "Your brothers have been here, but not you. You've met someone."

He couldn't help the big grin that spread over his face. "I have."

"Would it be the sweet little boy you knocked out in Sheila's place?"

He rolled his eyes. Trust the town gossips to have already spread the word. She'd probably heard it from Pablo.

"His name is Jack and he's very sweet."

"So tell me what he likes."

PJ licked his lips, and she narrowed her eyes.

"You haven't formalized this, have you? You're buying things just in case he agrees."

"I don't want to scare him off," PJ confessed.

"It's not like you to be worried about what a boy thinks. He must be special."

"He is special," PJ agreed. "He's into tigers and lions. Anything with big cats really but mainly tigers." PJ wouldn't have known if he hadn't spotted what decorated Jack's briefs.

"Do you want your usual?" she asked.

"I do, but twice the normal order."

Brenda laughed at him. "Your head may be unsure, but your heart has it all worked out."

"You really are a wicked woman," he said without rancor.

"And that's why you love coming to see me."

Brenda headed for a large closet PJ knew contained all her bolts of material. She opened the door and flicked on the light. A minute later she emerged with a green bolt of material under one arm and sky blue under the other. She displayed them to PJ. "Which one do you like best?"

PJ studied them both. "I think he'd like the green."

"He'd. Yes, I heard that. He's got you wrapped around his little finger."

PJ wanted to scoff but as usual Brenda was right. She looked after all the Daddies and boys in town. There was very little she didn't know.

"I'll get this started for you."

PJ bent to kiss her cheek. "Thanks, Brenda."

"When are your brothers back?"

"I don't know," he said.

"When Jake gets back, send him to see me."

PJ frowned. "Is everything all right? Is there anything I

can do to help?" He hated the thought that Brenda might need Jake's and Alec's services.

She blinked at him and then burst out laughing. "I'm fine, you silly boy. But thank you, you're a sweetheart to care."

PJ left, blinking in the afternoon sunshine. She really wasn't all there, he thought, as he headed for his truck. But she was a friend and in a town like theirs, friends who understood their lifestyle were precious.

He thought about going back to the bar again, but he didn't want to annoy Jack.

His boy. PJ couldn't hide his smile.

JACK

Jack glanced around at packing cases which littered the whole of the attic. "What am I looking for?"

PJ looked as helpless as he felt. "You said you were cold and needed a thicker coat."

This was true. He had said to PJ on the way home the previous night that he didn't realize how cold the nights were going to turn. He should have gotten a clue from the number of thick jackets hanging up in the hallway, even in the middle of summer. But he didn't have the money to pay for new clothes when he was still saving up for rent money.

"These boxes contain all our clothes from when we were babies onwards. My mom never threw anything out. You're welcome to look for a jacket from any of the boxes."

"You're all built like giants," Jack said.

PJ gave him an amused look. "We weren't born like this," he pointed out. "I didn't have a growth spurt until I hit my mid-teens. I just didn't stop growing."

"So somewhere here there's a pile of clothes from when you were my height?" Jack asked dubiously.

"Somewhere," PJ agreed. He looked around again with a hopeless expression. "Although I've got no idea where. I guess I could ask Lyle and Vinny as they walked away with nothing but the clothes on their back."

"All I want is a jacket," Jack said. "There's got to be one in a box somewhere. You start at one end, and I'll start at the other."

"Most of the boys have chosen clothes from their Daddy's old boxes."

Jack rolled his eyes. "You're nearly seven feet tall and I'm a foot and a half shorter. I'd probably have to pick clothes when you were eight."

It occurred to him that he might find clothes closer to his little age among the boxes. From the speculative glance PJ gave him, the same thought might have occurred to him too.

He started looking through the boxes. The earlier boxes were labeled, and it was easy to discard the baby clothes. Their mum had been meticulous at labeling which boy and what age, but he discovered that they all had hand-me-downs except Damien as he was the oldest. As they searched through each box, PJ told him tales of how they tried to blow up or destroy some of the clothes because they were so sick of wearing them.

"So that's where Brad got his hobby from," Jack said.

PJ looked startled. "I hadn't thought of that."

Jack found one dusty box labeled Outside Christmas Lights. He opened it up just to be nosy and found, unsurprisingly, strings of pretty Christmas lights and decorations. "I can't see anything to go on a Christmas tree."

PJ laughed. "By the time Christmas arrives we are sick of Christmas trees."

"I guess you must be."

"We decorate the outside of the cabin and Mom had decorations to go on the mantelpiece, but we don't really bother." PJ wrinkled his nose. "Maybe we ought to make more of an effort now we have boys in the house. Last Christmas we were too busy to really care."

"Do you think it'll come to an end now the theme parks are closing down?" Jack asked curiously.

PJ shrugged, then he rolled his shoulders. "I don't know, little one. I've never seen anything like this before."

Jack didn't want to pursue the pain in PJ's eyes. He opened another box and grinned. "I think I've struck gold. The entire box is full of jackets."

He pulled out one jacket and grimaced. "This would go down to my knees."

He held it against him, and PJ laughed.

"Yeah, no. They were mine after I had my growth spurt. Dig further down in the box. If I remember, the last time I looked in there, there were smaller ones at the bottom."

PJ's memory proved accurate, and Jack found two jackets that fitted him. They were well worn but he wasn't bothered, particularly when PJ told him they were both his. Jack liked the idea of wearing his Daddy's clothes.

"And this box contains hats and gloves and scarves," PJ said. "You'll need those as the weather gets colder."

Jack rummaged through the box and managed to find a set that weren't miles too big for him. "This was a good idea," he admitted. "Maybe I could find more jeans too."

It took several more boxes before PJ opened one to discover many pairs of jeans.

"You could open your own thrift store," Jack said.

"Then we wouldn't have anything to give our boys."

It was a good point. Jack had to delve down to the bottom before he found anything he could wear. But Jack didn't mind. Jeans were jeans and these didn't look too out of date. He was just grateful that he wouldn't have to keep doing laundry. One of the downsides to working in the bar was coming home smelling of beer.

"What would your mom say if she saw all the boys wearing these clothes?"

"She'd love it," PJ said dryly. "You have no idea how hard it was to get her to throw anything away."

"Your mom was a bit of a hoarder?"

"Define bit."

Jack chuckled. "My Gran is much the same."

"It's nice to hear you talk about your family," PJ said.

Jack stood with his new jacket and jeans. "You know in every family there is that uncle who always causes problems?"

PJ nodded fervently. "Uncle Chad. My mom's step-brother. Every year he'd get liquored up and start a fight at Christmas with my father. After my parents died, we stopped inviting him around. It was too stressful. Have you got an uncle like that?"

"I've got my Gran and my uncle. And he's a criminal."

Jack saw the moment PJ cottoned on.

"He's the one who's been sending you the messages."

Jack nodded. "I've got something of his and he wants it back."

"Why don't you change your cell phone number? We could buy you a new phone."

"Because it's my only connection to my grandmother. If I change the number, she's got no means of getting hold of me."

Jack didn't say that his Gran would be unlikely to ever ring him. There was always that possibility if she needed to and Jack couldn't take that away from her.

"I still think you need a new phone," PJ said dubiously. "You could block the phone number."

Jack gave him a wry smile. "He's calling from my Gran's phone because he knows it's the one number I'll never block." He swore he heard PJ growl under his breath. "It's okay, Daddy. He doesn't know where I am."

"Are you sure?"

Jack wasn't sure about anything, but he didn't want to worry PJ when he had so many other things on his mind. "My uncle is a small-town crook. He won't leave home to find me."

PJ didn't look convinced, but to Jack's relief he dropped the argument. Instead, he strode over to Jack and wrapped him in his arms. "I don't care what you took from him. You're never going back to him, do you understand?"

Jack couldn't hold PJ because of all the clothes he had in his arms, but he could reach out for a kiss. PJ gave a mighty groan in his throat and pressed his lips down on Jack's mouth. They kissed for a long while, until Jack's lungs protested that they needed air. He pulled back and PJ chased his mouth. "Need to breathe," he protested.

"Just one breath," PJ said. "I need to kiss you again." He went back to kissing Jack until Jack forgot what his own name was.

The cough was an unwelcome distraction. PJ pulled away and scowled at his brother.

"What?"

"I wondered where you two had gotten," Brad said.

Jack pulled back and caught the wicked grin on Brad's face.

PJ growled. "Go away. I'm busy."

"Get over yourself, little brother," Brad said. "Dinner's ready."

Jack could see PJ really wanted to tell Brad to fuck off, but he nodded curtly.

"We'll be down in a moment."

Brad dropped Jack a wink. "It's good to see my little brother looking so happy."

Jack couldn't help the smile spread across his face. He made PJ happy. What more could he want?

———

Jack had been at the cabin long enough to get his own set of chores. PJ, Brad, and Harry were more than happy to pass on most of the household work to him, despite his protests. He lived there, so he contributed to the household.

"I could find my own place in town," Jack pointed out when PJ presented him with the list on Jack's day off. Jack had planned to spend the day sleeping.

"You could," PJ agreed.

Bastard!

Jack looked down at the list. "You want me to clean the cabin."

"Just the downstairs and our rooms." PJ sounded way too cheerful.

"You're joking."

PJ shook his head. "Do you want to chop wood?"

Of course Jack didn't want to use the axe. He'd be more likely to chop his leg off.

Grumbling the whole way through, Jack worked through the cabin until he reached the top. He stripped the four beds and remade them with fresh linens. All the other bedrooms were ready for the brothers to come back.

The only room Jack hadn't been in was the one down the end. Jack poked his head around and his jaw dropped open. This wasn't a bedroom. It was a playroom, for little boys. He had never been in a room like it. All ideas of cleaning went out of his head as he looked around the room.

Toys were stored in boxes and put on the shelves. There was a large chair to sit in, just right for a Daddy and a boy. Most of the boxes were transparent and he could see cars and trains in them. But he went over to look at what was behind the cabinet doors.

He opened them up and stared, not quite believing his eyes. Diapers, sippy cups and pacifiers. He reached his hand out to touch them but pulled it back, knowing he wasn't allowed to touch other people's treasures.

"I wondered where you'd gone," PJ said.

6

PJ

PJ spent the morning away from the cabin. He took the opportunity to fill the woodstore. To be honest, he'd expected Jack to put up more of a fight about the list of chores. All the boys had mutinied at one point or another, except Aaron. It would be his turn when they came back. PJ grinned at the memory of Vinny's meltdown over the potatoes.

When he returned to the cabin the place was quiet. PJ furrowed his brow. He was sure preparing his lunch had been one of the chores.

"Jack?"

The cabin was still quiet, so PJ went on the hunt for him. Daddy Bear wasn't going to be pleased when he found his boy. PJ gleefully thought of punishments as he ran up the stairs. The bedrooms were empty although Jack had clearly cleaned them. There was only one other room left. PJ headed to the playroom, not surprised to find Jack looking through the drawers with the sippy cups and the pacifiers.

They hadn't had a talk about diapers yet. PJ added it to his things-to-do list.

"I wondered where you'd gone," he said. "If you'd wanted to know what was in here, you could have asked me."

Jack went bright red. "I didn't know about the room."

"This is the boys' playroom."

"I can see that," Jack said gravely.

"It used to be a bedroom." PJ didn't know why he was telling Jack that. It wasn't as if it meant anything to him. "Is there anything you like about the room?"

He should have introduced Jack to the room sooner, but they'd all been so busy, he hadn't had time to train the boy.

Jack swallowed hard. "I like the big chair. We could sit in that together."

PJ nodded. His brother had made the seats for everyone. They were big men, and they were made custom size. "I have one in my bedroom just like that." He flushed. "It's under a pile of my laundry."

Jack looked at him carefully. "I guess you hadn't had much need of the chair recently."

"That's right." PJ remembered telling Jack that he hadn't brought the boy home for a long time. He tended to play at the bar and take him to the motel if it was serious. He guessed it meant something that his first instinct had been to bring Jack home.

"But we could sit together in the chair," Jack said.

"Yes, we could."

PJ really needed to get past the awkward chitchat. He strode over to the chair, sat down, and held out his arms. Jack hesitated, then rushed over and sat on his lap, snuggling into his neck. PJ hugged him as close as he could. Jack smelled of cleaner and whatever body wash he'd used that morning.

"I like it here," Jack murmured.

PJ wasn't sure if he meant the cabin, the room, or in PJ's arms. But he didn't let Jack go, and Jack didn't seem in any hurry to move from his arms. "I like it here too."

"Perhaps you could teach me how to be a boy," Jack said. "I don't know what I'm doing."

PJ stroked Jack's hair. "I'm more than happy to teach you. Although we won't get much time in here when the boys are back. Gruff is teaching Lyle and Vinny how to read and write. They didn't get any education in the theme park. They're learning though."

"I can't believe they were treated so badly," Jack said.

"It's hard to believe," PJ agreed. "But every so often it hits you in the face."

They sat quietly for a long while until they heard Brad and Harry calling out for them.

PJ sighed. "You know they're just going to keep yelling until we answer them."

"I know." Jack's sigh was just as huge. "We'd better go find them."

But neither of them moved, content to stay in each other's arms.

"I can't wait for them to get their own boys," PJ muttered. "Then perhaps they will leave us alone."

"Do you really believe that?"

PJ gave a helpless laugh. "No not at all."

He kissed Jack on the top of the head and stood, gently placing Jack on the ground. He walked with Jack down the stairs and into the kitchen. Brad and Harry were making large sandwiches and arguing about something they had heard on the radio.

PJ expected hassle from Brad at least, but Harry drew them into the conversation about a shock jock on the local radio station. PJ knew him. He was less a shock and more wannabe jock, but he kept the locals entertained. Jack just sat and listened to them, seemingly amused.

"What do you think, Jack?" Harry demanded.

"I think he's never stepped outside the town and doesn't know what he's talking about," Jack said.

PJ waited for him to say more. After all, he hadn't been out of the town. But Jack left it there.

Harry grumbled but he nodded. "You're probably right."

"I need a night at the club," Brad groaned, changing the subject.

"I've got to work there tomorrow," Jack said. "If PJ could drive me down, would one of you drive me back?"

"I'll be there," PJ said sternly. "I'm not letting anyone like Earl Travis lay their hands on you again."

"He was just being an idiot," Brad said.

Jack agreed but PJ growled under his breath. He patted PJ's thigh. "Pablo says whoever does that to me again will be barred."

"But I won't be there and that's what's important."

PJ growled again. But he knew he was going to have to get over it if Jack was going to work there. He didn't have to like it though.

"Lyle messaged me," Harry said, clearly wanting to change the subject. "They've managed to close Columbus. It wasn't as bad as the others."

"Hopefully they'll be home soon," PJ said.

But Brad shook his head. "I spoke to Damien this morning. He said they won't be back for weeks. They've got to go to at least two more sites before they can come home."

"This is so wrong," Harry said.

"You said it, brother," PJ growled.

They were four daddies and four boys. What were they doing travelling the countryside, trying to rescue boys who needed help? And the worst thing was he and his brothers were not with them. They were stuck back at home taking care of the Christmas tree farm when their brothers were risking their lives.

JACK

Jack glanced between the three brothers. He'd never seen three men look so miserable. "When are they due back again?"

Brad shrugged. "Next month. Maybe the month after. None of us know." He got to his feet abruptly. "I'm gonna blow something up."

"Just make sure it's not the barn," Harry said. "It upsets the horses."

Brad stalked out, muttering under his breath.

Harry took his cup to the dishwasher. "You know where I'll be."

He vanished before anyone could respond, leaving Jack with PJ staring miserably into his cup.

"Daddy?" Jack said gently.

PJ looked up and Jack ached for the pain in his eyes. He wanted to sit on PJ's lap and kiss the pain away.

"It's okay, Jack. We get like this at times. It's hard for all of us, you know?"

Jack didn't know but he was beginning to understand.

"I'm gonna check the trees," PJ said and left just as abruptly as the others.

Were the trees upset by the explosions too?

Jack was hurt, but he knew PJ was hurting more. He sat

at the table alone for a long while, wondering what he could do to make PJ and his brothers feel better.

Then he had a germ of an idea. It was stupid. He might not even find what he was looking for. Maybe they'd laugh at him. But even laughing at Jack would be better than moping. Jack cleared away the dirty plates and headed to the attic.

He looked around the huge space and all the boxes and sighed. The family really needed to declutter the attic. He doubted they'd ever thrown anything away. Old televisions, kitchen equipment, clothes, and books. All of them piled high.

"Where was it?" he muttered. He knew he'd seen it when they looked for the jackets.

He wandered between the boxes. Some were labeled. 'Gruff's baby clothes.' 'Brad's prom suit.' 'PJ 8-9.'

Jack went over to have a look at PJ's box. Flannel shirts, T-shirts, and jeans. His lips twitched. His Daddy's fashion taste hadn't changed in nearly thirty years. Jack stroked one of the worn shirts. Maybe PJ would let Jack use part of one of his shirts as a comfort blanket.

But this wasn't going to help him find what he was looking for. Jack started at one end of the attic and worked his way down, looking in all the boxes. And then he spotted it. The huge square box with Outside Christmas Lights scrawled across it.

Jack sprang up and virtually skipped over to the box. He looked inside and broke into a huge smile. "This is what we need!"

First though, he needed his Daddy.

———

Jack wasn't sure where he'd find PJ. He wandered around the trees near the cabin. He didn't want to head into the trees because he wasn't sure he could find his way back.

As he walked into the yard, Jack spotted PJ by the mountain road. Perfect. He jogged over to him. "What are you doing here?" Jack asked.

PJ gave him a tight smile. "Just looking down the mountain road to see if I can see the buses."

Jack slipped his hand into PJ's. "Did you see anything?"

PJ shook his head. "Nothing. I know they're halfway across the country. It could be months before they return. But I still wait, just in case."

Jack took a deep breath and launched into his idea. "You've got a box upstairs in the attic full of outside Christmas lights."

PJ furrowed his brow. "Yeah. We put them around the cabin. Why?"

"What if we decorated the trees by the driveway? Is there anywhere to plug them in?"

"Uh...yeah. Why?" PJ looked confused.

Jack turned to PJ and wrapped his hands around PJ's jacket. "I know you're all upset. But I think you need to set a welcome for your brothers."

"A welcome?" PJ was plainly confused.

"Let's decorate the trees by the road." Jack held his breath, waiting for PJ's reaction.

PJ looked down the drive. "If we kept it on the whole time..."

"They'd know it was for them," Jack said softly.

"Where are the lights?"

Jack beamed at him. "In a box in the kitchen."

"You got them down." PJ looked bemused. "You did that for us?"

"I did it for you, Daddy," Jack corrected. "Because I want you to be happy."

PJ looked at the driveway again and then at Jack. He gave him an excited nod. "Let's find the others." He gathered Jack into a swift hug. "Thank you," he whispered.

They looked back to the cabin and went around the side of the house to find Harry and Brad. Harry was easy to find as he was in the barn with the horses.

Jack stayed back, leaving this to be a discussion between the two brothers.

PJ explained the idea to him, and Harry's eyes lit up.

"I think that's a great idea. Are the lights in the attic?"

PJ shook his head. "They're in the kitchen now."

Harry shot a look at Jack and then to PJ. "Have you told Brad?"

"Not yet. We'll be by the trees in fifteen minutes," PJ said. "We'll drag Brad out of the barn now."

"Go easy," Harry said. "He's not stopped exploding things since he went in the barn."

PJ grimaced. "He must be feeling really bad. I'll get Brad. You and Jack bring the lights."

Jack shook his head. "*I'll* get Brad. We'll meet you by the trees."

Harry wasn't wrong about the number of explosions. Jack grimaced, feeling sympathy for the poor horses who had to listen to this. He knocked on the barn door as loudly as he could. He wasn't stepping a foot inside that barn.

The explosions paused.

"What?" Brad snapped.

"It's Jack. Your brothers need you."

Maybe it was a bit unfair not to give him the information, but Brad could be stubborn. Jack sat down on an old log and waited for Brad to come out. A few seconds later the door opened, and Brad emerged, wearing safety glasses and a mask, and covered in soot. Jack coughed at the soot that wafted from the barn.

"What do you mean they need me?" Brad insisted. "What happened?"

"Come with me," Jack said.

He didn't give Brad time to think, as he led him around the cabin and down the driveway.

PJ and Harry were already there, pulling the strings of lights out of the box.

PJ looked up as Brad approached. "What do you think about this one on the bottom?" He held it up.

"I've got no idea what you're talking about," Brad snarled. "Jack said you needed me."

PJ looked at Jack who just shrugged.

"You can explain. I'm going back to finish the chores."

He left them alone, the three brothers, hoping this worked. He couldn't think of any other way to make them happy.

It was nearly six when the door opened, and PJ walked in. There was no sign of the other two. PJ looked tired, but relaxed.

"Is it done?" Jack asked.

"All done," PJ agreed. "When the sun goes down, I'll take you to have a look."

"Where are the other two?"

"They're arguing about how best to power it. As long as Brad doesn't blow anything up, I've left them to it."

PJ walked over to Jack and swept him into his arms. "Thank you, little one. You have no idea how much that means to the three of us."

"I didn't know what else to do," Jack confessed. "You were all so miserable."

"It's the first thing they'll see when they come up the mountain road," PJ said. "Damien will bitch about the electricity and Jake will be concerned about fire, but they'll know it was for them."

"That's all that matters." Jack buried himself against PJ and accepted the hug. He'd done good.

As darkness fell, PJ nudged Jack toward the rack of coats in the hall. They shrugged into their jackets and stomped into their boots. PJ took Jack's hand and led him out of the cabin.

Jack hadn't spent much time out of the cabin that day and it was good to suck in the fragrant evening air.

PJ wrapped his beefy arm around Jack's shoulders as they walked down the driveway. "I never thought we'd have lights to welcome someone home."

Jack looked up at him. "Everyone needs a guiding light to know which way is home."

7

PJ

PJ frowned as he spotted the lights making their way up the mountain road. The rusty old pickup turned into the driveway for the cabin and stopped. A moment later Jack joined PJ by the twinkling tree lights.

"I thought I'd find you here," his boy said, reaching up for a kiss.

PJ brushed his lips over Jack's and wrapped his arm around Jack's shoulders. "I always wait for my loved ones to arrive."

He spent hours by the trees, looking down the mountain road for any lights. He knew it was pointless waiting for the RVs. Damien had told him he didn't know when they'd be home, but it didn't stop PJ standing vigil. He'd met Brad and Harry here too, peering down the mountain road. But PJ also waited for an old rusty pickup to return to him each day and smiled in relief when he saw the lights approaching him.

"How was your day?" PJ asked. "And why are you here? I thought you were working tonight?"

Jack grimaced. "Pablo's asked me to work Tuesday night instead, so he let me go early."

PJ frowned. "I thought he understood you weren't gonna work Daddy and boys night."

Earl Travis hadn't been the only one who'd tried to claim his boy. One out-of-town Daddy had proved very insistent. Harry had been at the bar at the time, and they'd nearly come to blows. His brother had a fierce right hook. The out-of-town Daddy was lucky Pablo intervened.

"He was desperate, and I need the money. So I said yes."

"I'll be there," PJ said.

"You don't have to—"

"I do have to!" PJ insisted and Jack cuddled in close to him.

"I'm glad. I wasn't looking forward to it."

PJ was going to have a word with Pablo about the shift switch, but at least he'd be there to ward off any handsy Daddies. PJ knew a lot of Daddies liked sweet twinks like his boy, but Jack was firmly taken.

They piled into the pickup and as he drove the short distance to the cabin, Jack said "I don't know if I should tell you this, but Harry's spending a lot of time at the bar and he's drinking. If I'm not there to drive him back, he stays at the motel."

"That doesn't sound like Harry," PJ said, furrowing his brow. Harry drank liquor rarely and he went to the Tin Bar to hook-up.

"He doesn't want to be here, Daddy."

PJ got it. Jack was very perceptive. His older brother was lonely and hurting. He'd watch Harry carefully. Maybe he'd spend more time at the bar. PJ had been avoiding the bar to give Jack his space. But Jack needed his Daddy and Harry needed his brother, so PJ would step up. At least, Brad was taking his pain out on the barn. He had to rebuild it when he went too far which kept him at home.

"Is Harry at the bar now?" he asked.

"No."

PJ squinted at Jack's terse response. "What am I missing?"

"He knows you wait for me by the lights. I dropped him further down the road. He'll be back soon."

"Maybe I should meet him."

Jack laid a hand on PJ's arm. "Not tonight, Daddy. Harry said he's gonna head to the barn. He needs his space."

PJ hated the thought his brother wanted time alone, but he trusted Jack's judgement. "I've cooked your dinner if you're hungry."

"It's the only thing I think about when I drive home," Jack said.

"Me cooking your dinner?"

Jack snorted. "Being here with you."

"I need you too, my boy. We're going to eat. Then I'm gonna give you tub time and I'm gonna cuddle my little in the big chair."

Jack sighed happily. "That sounds perfect."

Inside the cabin, PJ slipped Jack's coat off his shoulders, and pushed him down so he could take off Jack's boots. He saw the lines of tension ease from around Jack's eyes as he settled into his little.

"Let's go eat, little one."

"Daddy, I wanna wear my onesie."

PJ shook his head. "After your bath." He hid his grin as Jack jutted out his bottom lip, but he didn't want the boy to think he was a soft touch. "You don't want to make the onesie dirty, do you?"

Jack still pouted but he nodded. "Yes, Daddy."

"We're gonna wash your hands first. Make them all clean and shiny for dinner."

PJ took Jack over to the sink and rubbed soap over his hands, then guided them under the water to rinse them. PJ dried Jack's hands, then pointed to the table. "Sit down, little one."

Jack sat in his chair and PJ brought over his plate of food. Usually, Jack was too tired after a day at the bay to regress into his little, so PJ left him to eat and decompress in his own time. But today Jack was back early enough that they could have fun.

PJ smiled at his boy as he tucked a green bib around Jack's neck. "I'm gonna feed my sweet boy today."

Jack touched the bib with one finger. "This fits me, Daddy, and it's got big tigers."

"That's because it's made for my sweet boy."

Brenda had delivered his items that day and Jack had gotten away early. It was fate.

"Thank you, Daddy." Jack's eyes lit up as he saw the plate covered in lions and tigers. He touched the head of one of the tigers. "Did you buy this for me too?"

"I did, baby. Just for you. And I have a cup to match."

PJ poured milk into the green sippy cup with matching lions and tigers. His boy wasn't having coffee. Not tonight.

His boy took the cup happily and sucked on it. He smiled a milky smile when he put the cup down.

PJ slowly fed him. Jack grumbled at eating his vegetables, but he subsided when PJ gave him a piece of carrot to hold in each hand. PJ was learning fast that Jack liked holding things. His cock twitched at the thought of Jack's small hand around it.

By the time Jack crunched the last stick of carrot, he declared his tummy was full. PJ was more than happy with that. He cleared away the dinner plates and was ready to get on with the next part of the evening.

PJ took Jack up to his bedroom, stripped off his clothes, and wrapped him in a big, fluffy towel. "You sit in the big chair while I fill the tub." He handed Jack his pacifier.

Jack stared at it, then he looked up at PJ. "Daddy, wanna a new Binky."

"What do you say?"

Jack pouted. "Please?"

"You can, little one," PJ said. "You can pick one from the playroom."

Jack gave him the sweetest smile which was spoiled by a sudden yawn. "Not today. I'm so tired."

"I'll put you to bed after this."

"I don't want to be alone," Jack sulked, jamming his Binky in his mouth.

"You're gonna sleep in my bed from now on," PJ assured him. "My boy only sleeps with his Daddy."

He loved Jack's full body shiver.

PJ filled the tub with bubbles. When he returned to his bedroom, Jack was dozing in the chair. "Come on, little one. Time to make you all clean for your Daddy."

Jack wrapped his arms around PJ's neck and let PJ take him into the bathroom, resting his head against PJ, but he cried out with happiness when he saw the tub filled with bubbles and toys.

"You can play with the toys for a few minutes," PJ said as he helped Jack into the tub.

Jack sank down into the water until it reached his chin. "Yes, Daddy."

PJ let him play with the toys before he took a washcloth and rubbed it over his boy. Jack grumbled because he still wanted to play. PJ leaned forward to give him a kiss for being such a good boy and Jack smacked his hand down, splashing PJ in the face.

PJ stared at Jack, water running down his face and into his beard. Jack giggled and covered his mouth.

Oh ho, his little boy could be bratty too. PJ held back his grin. "My little boy is being naughty."

"I'm sorry, Daddy."

PJ might have believed him if Jack hadn't giggled again. "I don't like boys who are naughty."

The humor faded from Jack's eyes and in his place was something PJ couldn't quite place. Fear? Excitement?

"I'm going to put you over my knees and spank your bottom."

PJ said it carefully, watching for Jack's reaction. One of their boys, Vinny, had been severely beaten as a child, and Damien refused to spank him or allow it around him. But the only thing PJ saw in Jack's eyes was excitement.

Jack licked his lips. "Yes, Daddy. Sorry, Daddy."

PJ kissed the top of Jack's wet hair. His boy was so good.

JACK

Jack couldn't contain his excitement as PJ dried him with the fluffy towel.

"Stand still, boy," PJ growled.

Jack hung his head. "I'm sorry, Daddy."

PJ rubbed him down making sure every nook and cranny of Jack was dry. It seemed to take forever. Jack wanted to beg him to hurry up, but he knew his Daddy was in charge. PJ dusted him down with powder, then PJ folded the towel and put it over the towel rail.

Come on, come on, come on. Jack was desperate now.

Then PJ took Jack's hand and led him to the big chair. Usually the chair was covered in PJ's flannel shirts and clean laundry, but now it was empty and ready for use.

PJ sat down and looked at his beautiful naked boy. He had little body hair and the small patches under his arms and around his cock were the lightest blond. "Why am I going to give you a spanking, little one?" He never delivered any punishment without his boy knowing why.

"Because I splashed you in the face," Jack said, as contritely as he could.

PJ nodded, his expression solemn. "I don't let little boys be rude to me. Over my lap," he ordered.

Jack placed himself over PJ's knees, finding it awkward and not sure what position he was supposed to be in, other than ass up. PJ placed his large hands on him and maneuvered him where he wanted Jack. Blood rushed to Jack's head and his limbs seem to dangle awkwardly over PJ's lap. Jack hissed as his hardening cock was trapped beneath him.

"This won't be a hard spanking," PJ assured him. "You were only being playful."

Jack wasn't entirely sure why he was getting a spanking, but as PJ laid his large hand on Jack's ass, it occurred to him that maybe PJ wanted to spank him as much as he wanted to be spanked.

PJ seemed to cover his ass with his hand and then suddenly pain shot through Jack as PJ smacked him, taking Jack's breath away. If this wasn't a hard spanking, Jack wasn't sure what was. The next smack wasn't as forceful, and Jack could breathe through it. He wriggled and hissed as his cock hardened underneath him.

"My little boy isn't allowed to come," PJ warned.

Jack turned to look at him. "You're joking?"

PJ raised an eyebrow and Jack realized he really wasn't joking. He didn't know how he was going to get through this without coming all over his Daddy's lap. He knew PJ was just as hard. He could feel the thick shaft underneath him.

Eight more spanks, then PJ rested his hand on Jack's flaming ass.

"That's enough, for now. Your ass blushes so prettily."

PJ helped Jack to his feet. Jack swayed as the blood rushed from his head, but PJ made sure Jack didn't fall over. PJ stood, running his hands down Jack's sides, then cupping his ass so that Jack hissed.

"I want to take my boy to bed," PJ said, and Jack knew from the look in his eyes that if Jack said no, PJ would abide by it.

"I'd like that," he said shyly.

"You make me very happy, little one."

PJ led Jack to his large bed and pulled down the covers. Then he picked Jack up and laid him on his side. Jack was confused until he realized he'd suddenly received a spanking.

PJ stripped off his clothes and laid his big furry body beside Jack. He pushed Jack's hair back from his face and looked at him. "We are learning about each other. I don't know whether you want to fuck in your little mode, but I'll do whatever you want."

Jack hesitated. "I've never..."

"As a little?" PJ asked, his expression kind.

"Ever," Jack whispered, embarrassed to have to admit this was his first time in bed with any man.

"You honor me, little one," PJ said. "I promise I'll take care of you."

Jack wondered how he could have been so lucky to find a huge bear who treated him as if he were his world. When he remembered what he could have ended up with, PJ was a revelation.

PJ stretched over him, careful not to press Jack into the mattress, and kissed him. The kiss started out as chaste and gentle, but quickly became more heated when Jack parted his lips. They kissed for long moments until Jack couldn't help the thrust of his hips into PJ. He wanted more. PJ slid his hand down Jack's back, gently brushed his hot ass, and then round to enfold Jack's cock in his warm hand. Jack held onto PJ's shoulders as PJ tugged him.

"I'm not going to last much longer if you carry on with that," Jack confessed.

PJ smiled and kissed him once more, then he reached out to his nightstand and pulled out lube and condoms. He squeezed lube into his fingers and gently parted Jack's legs. The cool lube on Jack's spanked flesh made him gasp, but then his whole focus zeroed down to the finger rubbing around his hole. Nothing else mattered, except the finger which pressed in gently. Jack hissed at the burn but when PJ stopped, he begged him to carry on. PJ took his time, and then one finger became two. Jack nearly yelled when PJ grazed his sweet spot. PJ thrust in again and Jack arched as PJ brushed his prostate. Jack clutched at the sheets as PJ continued to prepare him, two fingers becoming three. He didn't stop no matter how much Jack said he was ready.

"I'm a big guy," PJ said when Jack protested for the third time. "I don't want to hurt you."

Finally, Jack knew he couldn't wait any more. "Please, please, hurry up."

PJ nodded, and Jack moaned as PJ withdrew his fingers. "Not long now, little one." Then PJ was over him, pushing Jack's knees up to his chest. His boy's pretty hole waited for him.

Jack cried out as PJ breached him. "Wait," he gasped.

PJ stilled, not moving, not breathing, his eyes fixed on his boy, until Jack was able to let out a breath. "I'll wait as long as you need me to," he assured Jack.

Jack sucked in a shaky breath and stared into PJ's blue eyes. "I'm okay now."

PJ took his time, easing himself inside Jack's clenching channel. He waited until Jack nodded again, then he pulled back and thrust into him. Jack had been waiting on a knife edge for so long it didn't take him long to climax, shooting white heat over the sheets. PJ kissed Jack fiercely as he trembled through the aftershocks, then two or three fierce thrusts and PJ was done, Jack feeling him shudder as he emptied into the condom.

Jack held his Daddy as their breaths calmed, his fingers trailing through Jack's wild hair. PJ sighed and snuggled closer.

"Thank you, Daddy." Jack murmured, smiling as PJ snored gently.

———

The Tin Bar was busy, and Jack didn't have time to think. He served drinks and cleared tables. Rinse. Repeat.

"Thanks for saving my ass, kid," Pablo said, partway through the evening. "I'm gonna kill that kid for letting me down again."

'That kid' was Pablo's nephew who took full advantage of being related to the boss by doing as little as possible. Jack just nodded and kept his mouth shut. He knew better than to criticize a member of Pablo's family.

Pablo glanced PJ's way. "You know he never takes his eyes off you."

Jack looked up occasionally to make sure his Daddy was there, and he was, all the time, watching him. PJ sat with Harry and Brad, but he only watched Jack. "I know," Jack said.

"You've quit denying you're a boy, then?" Pablo asked.

Jack just smiled at him and went to serve a boy. His Daddy was his business. No one else's.

It hadn't been easy working with PJ staring at him all night. Jack had been ready to kill anyone who went near his Daddy. To Jack's relief, PJ refused all the offers from the sweet twinks, instead sending them to Brad and Harry. His lap was clear all night, just for Jack.

No one came near Jack all night. Not one Daddy laid a finger on his butt. PJ had laid an invisible forcefield around him and he could breathe as he walked through the bar to clear the tables.

The small blond little PJ had rolled the ball to waved at him as he walked past. Jack waved at him too. Ian was a sweet kid, despite the fact he was some multi-millionaire hotshot pop artist. Ian had confessed to him they liked it here, because no one knew who the hell he was. He was Daddy Graham's little. That's all they cared about.

Jack had thought about that for a long while. He couldn't imagine being in the public eye. All he wanted was to be in his Daddy's arms in that safe cabin on the mountainside. He wondered if PJ would prefer a famous boy like Ian, rather than a penniless guy like him.

Jack walked over to PJ's table with his tray. The two twinks gave him suspicious looks but they relaxed when he made it clear he didn't want their Daddies for the night. He only had eyes for *his* Daddy. He squawked as PJ pulled him onto his lap.

Pablo looked up, a frown between his brows, then he rolled his eyes as he saw Jack on PJ's lap. "Let my bartender go."

PJ drew Jack in a long and lingering kiss, then patted his butt. He smirked as Jack hissed.

"You're mean, Daddy," Jack grumbled, but he pressed his butt against PJ's hand.

PJ gave it a light squeeze. Jack gasped again. Then PJ placed Jack on his feet. "You'd better get to work, boy."

Jack huffed, but he did as he was told. He didn't think his ass would take another spanking. At least, not tonight. He wriggled in his jeans. His Daddy's hand on his butt had been so hot.

"Little one?"

Jack jumped as PJ broke into his thoughts. He glanced around to see PJ's concerned expression, but worse, Harry and Brad grinning at him. His cheeks flamed and he rushed away with the tray before he got himself into more trouble.

8

PJ

The booming engine noise woke PJ. He raised his head in concern, not sure what was happening. It was like the chalet was shaking. It didn't seem to have disturbed Jack, who was still pressed into his arms, his butt pressed against PJ's groin.

PJ squinted at his phone. It was only just after two in the morning. They'd been asleep for less than an hour after getting home from the club. No wonder he felt exhausted. He listened intently for a moment and then a voice rang out.

"Is anyone awake?"

There was only one person that could be. PJ couldn't help the broad smile across his face. He eased himself away from Jack who grumbled but settled back down. PJ tiptoed to the window and opened it.

"Shut the fuck up, noisy assholes," he bellowed.

Damien grinned up at him. "Two dollars! I thought we'd be getting a proper welcome."

"And you would have been, if you bothered to tell us when you were turning up," PJ pointed out. "You could have arrived in the daylight." He grinned at his brother, feeling the tension ease in his gut for the first time since the taillights of the RV's had vanished months ago. "It's damn good to see you again, big brother."

"Likewise," Damien boomed. "Get your ass down here now."

PJ shut the window and turned to find Jack blinking owlishly at him. "Sorry to wake you up, little one."

"What's happening?" Jack asked around a yawn.

"My brothers are back." PJ could not erase the smile from his face. "I'm going to check they're in one piece. You can go back to sleep if you want."

Jack sat up, looking surprised and nervous. "Your brothers? They're back already? I thought they weren't due back for months."

PJ skinned into a thick Aran sweater and sweatpants, then sat on the bed to roll on his socks. "I guess they wanted to surprise us." He looked at Jack. "Just let me say hello to them and then I'll come back," he promised.

Jack shook his head and rubbed his eyes. "You say hello. I'll be down in a minute."

PJ smiled at his boy and charged out of his bedroom, bellowing for Brad and Harry to get up. He heard grumpy cursing from Brad. "They're back! They're all back!"

He didn't bother to see if Brad and Harry understood.

PJ took the stairs two at a time. He was just about to fling open the door when it opened in his face. PJ was lucky not to land on his ass.

Jake stood in the doorway. PJ opened his mouth to grumble at his brother, but then he was gathered into the biggest bearhug Jake had ever given him. Jake stuck his head on PJ's shoulder and sobbed in his arms. PJ held him close and let his own tears fall.

They were home. His brothers were home.

But it wasn't just Jake. Then Damien was there. His big brother was the soppiest creature who ever lived so he was crying too. Brad was at his back, howling, and Harry, who must have been already up, ran from the barn, straight into Gruff's arms. They all ended up in the kitchen, hugging each other, and all the brothers joined them, Alec grabbing Brad and blubbing into his robe. Seven brothers who should never have been apart, crying in each other's arms.

PJ didn't care. He finally had his brothers back again and that's all he cared about. He reeled in Damien for a hug.

"I missed you, big brother," he whispered, tears running into his beard.

"Missed you too, you ass," Damien sobbed into his shoulder.

Then it was Gruff's turn, and his youngest brother was crying as hard as he was. Gruff had lost weight. He was still a big man, but that comfortable 'bearness' wasn't there.

Slowly the brothers disentangled but stayed close. Good, because PJ wasn't letting any of them out of his sight.

"Why didn't you tell me you were coming back?" he demanded. "I spoke to you last night."

Gruff, who looked thin and exhausted, said "We took a vote. And we all voted to come back home."

PJ hugged him once again. "I'm so glad you did." Fresh tears spilled on his cheeks to get lost in his beard.

"Whose idea was it for the tree?" Alec asked.

"Uh...my boy, Jack. We were all struggling, and he suggested we decorated the tree by the road, to give you a light home."

"We saw it from a distance," Damien said. "We didn't

know what it was, but we knew it came from our home. How much...you know what, it doesn't matter. The lights were perfect. You can switch them off now though."

"We were gonna stop in town and drive up in the morning, but we saw the lights and decided home was more important," Jake agreed.

PJ needed to thank Jack again for his idea. And then he'd spank him, just because.

Gruff looked around. "Where is your boy? I want to meet him."

"I think he's given us time to reconnect." PJ said. "Where are your boys?"

Gruff shrugged. "Probably trying to avoid seven howling bears."

Then PJ was being hugged again by Alec and Jake and Damien. It didn't escape his notice that each of his brothers had lost weight and looked as if their worlds had fallen apart. He would do everything in his power to take that look away. And if any of them decided they were leaving, he would bar the fucking driveway. He was never going through this again.

"Get your boys in," he ordered. "It's too cold out there. Brad, hot chocolate for everyone."

Usually his brothers would have grumbled at PJ ordering them around. But Brad headed for the stovetop and Alec jogged over to the door to yell for the boys to come in.

If the brothers looked bad, PJ wanted to weep at the sight of the four boys. Lyle looked haunted, like the boy Gruff had found in the snow. But they looked as if they'd been through hell, even Aaron, who'd never been part of the Kingdom theme parks. They needed as much TLC as his brothers.

He hugged each one gently, told them how pleased he was to see them back in their home. Even Matt who'd never really lived here. Matt shook in his arms and hugged him closer.

"You're not leaving, okay?" PJ whispered in his ear because Matt had a habit of taking off home without telling anyone. But this time Matt just nodded.

A squeak on the floorboards made him look around and he saw Jack glowering at him. He realized that he'd been caught holding one of his brother's boys.

PJ patted Matt's back and stood back, smiling at Jack. "Come meet my brothers and their boys, Jack." He held out his hand. Jack hesitated and then joined him. PJ saw his eyes go wide as he glanced around the seven brothers.

"The gay daddy bear convention," Jack muttered.

PJ barked out a laugh. "You're right there."

He was aware the conversation had suddenly died, and everyone was looking at the two of them. He rolled his eyes. "Jack, these are my brothers. The grumpy one is Damien. He's the oldest. You have to pay attention to him because he's old. Gruff is the youngest. You can ignore everything he says." He grinned as Gruff spluttered. Jack leaned into him for comfort. PJ put his arm around him and hauled Jack against him. "This is my boy, Jack. We're still working things out so don't hassle him or me."

"Good to finally meet you," Lyle said, coming forward to hold out his hand to Jack. "PJ has not stopped talking about you."

PJ knew he was blushing as Jack looked up at him.

"You told them about me?" Jack sounded surprised as if he thought PJ would hide him.

"Of course I told them about you," he grumbled.

"There are no secrets in this house," Lyle told Jack. "The brothers are incapable of hiding anything from each other."

"You're not supposed to say that out loud," Gruff protested.

Lyle raised an eyebrow. "You think it's something you can hide. How sweet."

Gruff's boy had obviously spent far too much time in Vinny's company. He was a lot more feisty than before.

Jack looked overwhelmed so PJ ordered everyone to sit down.

"You've gotten bossy," Alec muttered.

PJ told him to shut the fuck up and yes, he'd pay the dollar. He'd pay a thousand dollars just to have his brothers back with him again.

Brad served the hot chocolate to everyone, and PJ watched as his four brothers and their boys relaxed. It was probably the first time any of them had taken a breath since they left.

Jack had not let go of PJ's hand and his other hand was in his pocket, almost certainly clutched around his Binky. PJ knew it had to be hard for Jack to be suddenly confronted with the Brenner family in its entirety. He drew Jack onto his lap and enfolded him in his arms. Jack hesitated at first but then he saw Lyle and Aaron on their Daddy's laps, and even Vinny was pressed up close to Damien. PJ looked at Matt. He looked almost asleep as he leaned against Alec.

"I know this is overwhelming," PJ murmured in Jack's ear. "But don't be scared. You can stay by my side. I won't let go of you, little one."

JACK

Jack clutched onto PJ's hand as he watched the chaos swirl around him. All the brothers talked at the top of their voices, cuddling their boys. He wasn't used to the noise. If he had thought the house was full with two other brothers, it was nothing like having all seven brothers and five boys in the kitchen. It was deafening as they all talked over each other. But for the first time PJ seemed truly happy and Jack understood what his family meant to him. PJ didn't need him now his brothers had returned.

But PJ kept his promise. He didn't let go of Jack. Jack buried his face in PJ's shoulder, aware of the curious glances from all of them, especially the boys, but he wasn't ready to face them yet.

There was more talking, more hot chocolate, and Jack petted the dog who'd suddenly appeared. One of the boys told him his name was Rexy. He'd made it clear Rexy was *his* dog. That was fine with Jack. He'd never had a pet.

Jack listened in horror to some of the stories about the theme parks they'd had to visit, and the condition of the boys they'd had to rescue. There were more than a few tears shed and Jack understood why the sweet-looking boy seemed so haunted.

Jack made a vow to himself that he would treat Lyle, Vinny and Matt with special care, and Aaron too because although he'd been on the fringe of the action, he'd had to listen to them talk about it every single day.

It was nearly five in the morning before they returned to bed. The brothers had talked themselves hoarse. Jack was thankful that he didn't have to work the next day. He didn't care if Pablo begged him on his knees to come in, there was no way he was leaving PJ.

PJ guided him into his bedroom, and they stripped off their clothes and tumbled into bed, wrapping their arms around each other.

PJ gave an unexpected rumble of laughter and Jack raised his head to find out what he was laughing about.

"Alec and Matt," PJ explained. "Matt used to insist he slept in the small room, but he went straight into Alec's room without a protest. I wonder if they're going to admit they're together."

Jack smiled but he didn't care about them. He only cared about the man in his arms.

PJ stroked down Jack's back and cupped his ass. "I love you being here with me."

Jack melted into him, but he had worries. "Would you prefer me to move into town now your brothers have returned?"

PJ frowned. "You're not going anywhere."

"You don't want to keep driving me up and down to town, and Jake is back now. He'll need his pickup."

"I've been thinking about that," PJ rumbled. "Tomorrow we'll buy you a car of your own."

"I can't afford that," Jack said horrified.

"One of my customers is selling his old pickup," PJ explained. "It's a rust bucket but it keeps going and he doesn't want much for it. I think he's grateful to be rid of it. And it's good on these roads. I said we'd go and look at it tomorrow — today."

Jack relaxed. It didn't matter that it was an old vehicle. He could save the money to pay back PJ.

He relaxed against PJ's furry chest. The soft hair tickled his cheek, but it was comforting. He didn't think he would ever want to sleep alone again.

"I like your brothers," he whispered. "I see what you mean now."

"Mean about what, little one?"

"About being gay daddies. It's so obvious when you see all of you together."

He heard PJ rumble a laugh underneath him. "Just wait until you see us all in the Tin Bar."

"I've heard enough about you," Jack said. "Some of the twinks never stop talking about the fabulous Brenner brothers."

Jack had almost put his job on the line after one boy would not stop drooling over PJ. If Pablo hadn't told the boy to go away, Jack would have had to admit to PJ that he no longer had a job because he was ready to punch the boy. PJ was his and only his.

PJ held him closer. "And yet there's a reason we all picked boys from out of town."

Jack felt the knot of tension ease in his chest. He needed to take PJ at his word and trust him. "Love you, Daddy."

"I love you too, little one."

It took a while for Jack to relax, but he listened to PJ's breathing even out and the slow rumbling snore begin. Jack wasn't even sure he was that tired now, but he didn't want to move away from PJ.

A stripe of moonlight covered the duvet from a crack in the drapes. It reminded him he could have been sleeping rough if it hadn't been for the kindness of this huge man. One of the things he learned about PJ from the twinks in the bar was that PJ never committed to anyone. What was the difference about him? Why had PJ taken a chance on him? He would need to ask that question.

———

The stripe of moonlight had been replaced by bright sunlight in Jack's eyes. He groaned as he opened his eyes and buried his face in his pillow. He reached out to hug PJ but came up empty. Jack cracked one eye open to discover he was alone in the bed. Disappointed, Jack listened, not surprised to hear talking from downstairs. He smiled when he heard PJ's laugh boom out. His Daddy was happy.

Jack rolled onto his back and stared up at the ceiling. He wasn't ready to face the Brenners *en masse* yet. He needed a hot shower first. Jack climbed out of bed and headed into the bathroom. The shower was just what he needed. Jack closed his eyes and let the water stream over him.

"Now that's a lovely sight," PJ rumbled.

Jack blinked away the water and saw PJ in the doorway. "You like what you see?" Yes, he preened at the sight of his Daddy staring at him with frank admiration.

"You know I do," PJ said.

Jack couldn't hide the fact his cock hardened and rose as if it was seeking PJ's touch. "Do you want to wash me, Daddy?" He offered himself to his Daddy, making it clear that his body was for PJ's pleasure.

PJ folded his arms and shook his head. His chest and arms were massive. "I think my boy ought to get out here."

Jack shut off the water and stepped out of the shower. PJ immediately wrapped him up in a large, warm, fluffy towel. Jack murmured his appreciation as PJ dried him from head to foot. His murmurs turned into a groan as PJ pressed against his shaft, then slid the towel down to cup his balls.

Before Jack could ask what PJ wanted him to do, PJ dropped the towel, lifted Jack in his arms and took him into the bedroom, gently putting him on the bed.

"I need you," Jack said and held out his arms.

His Daddy gave him a tender smile. "You know just what to say to me."

He stripped off his clothes, his thick cock slapping on his belly as he pulled off his sweats and got onto the bed beside Jack.

Jack made a mew of dissatisfaction. "I want you over me," he insisted.

"And I'm not about to squash my boy," PJ said with a sternness that thrilled Jack.

He'd never admit it but he loved his Daddy going all Daddy bear on his ass. He couldn't wait for PJ to put him over his knees and spank his butt again. That had been so hot. Perhaps he should be naughty again.

PJ tugged him closer. "I love you, little one. And I want to take care of you forever."

"I'd like that," Jack whispered.

PJ propped himself up on one elbow and ran his hand down Jack's body. "It's time I showed my boy just how much I love him."

He pressed a sweet kiss to Jack's lips. Then he ran his tongue along the seam of Jack's mouth, requesting admittance. Jack parted his lips willingly and PJ pressed his tongue in. Their tongues slid together in a mating dance and PJ groaned as he pulled Jack on top of him.

Jack didn't know how long they kissed for, but his lungs were burning when PJ finally pulled back. Then PJ pressed him into the mattress again and kissed a trail of hot wet kisses along his jawline and down his neck. He sucked briefly on Jack's Adam's apple, then carried on pressing his lips to Jack's pulse point. He kissed down the center of Jack's sternum then diverted to explore each nipple, making it wet and hard. Jack groaned and arched his hips, but PJ was too strong and pressed him back into the pillow.

PJ continued his exploration of Jack's body, telling him he was perfect at every new shiver he elicited. Jack had never been worshiped like this before. PJ didn't leave an inch of Jack undiscovered. He explored Jack's bellybutton, then followed the thin trail down to the neat hairs around his leaking cock.

PJ licked from route to tip, dipping into the slit, and groaning happily at the taste of Jack's pre-come. Jack clutched at the sheet, pushing his hips up into PJ's willing, eager, mouth.

"You taste so good," PJ murmured and dipped back down for another taste.

Jack closed his eyes. He had to keep control, but if PJ kept doing this to him it would be the shortest blow job in history. PJ didn't seem to realize the effect he was having on Jack and swirled his tongue around the glans. Jack wanted to clutch his hair, beg him to stop, give Jack a chance to regain control. But he was worried if he did that PJ would pull away for good.

"Jack! PJ!"

The shout broke into Jack's stupor. He raised his head as someone, he wasn't sure who, yelled for them.

PJ frowned, obviously annoyed at their lovemaking being disturbed. "What?" he bellowed.

"There's someone here to talk to Jack. He says he's Jack's uncle."

And with one word, Jack's perfect world shattered into nothing.

9

PJ

"We'll be down in a minute, Brad," PJ yelled, annoyed at having his time with his boy disrupted.

"Okay," Brad said.

PJ was about to sit up when he saw Jack's wide-eyed panic. "Hey, what's wrong, little one?"

"I've got to get away from here." Jack struggled to sit up, but PJ rolled over and trapped Jack underneath him. Jack tried to push him away. "You've got to let me go."

"Jack, it's okay," PJ assured him, pushing Jack's hair back from his face.

"You don't understand."

No, PJ didn't, because Jack hadn't told him the full story, but he remembered Jack's description of his uncle. Well, his uncle was going to learn was it was to be faced with the Brenners.

"Let me go, Daddy," Jack begged. "It's not safe."

Jack fought to get free, and his wiry strength was

stronger than PJ expected, but PJ used his bulk to keep Jack where he was, safe in his arms. He could see Jack was lost in his fear, unable to focus on anything except his panic.

"I've got you, little one. You're safe," PJ said soothingly. He repeated the words again until he saw the panic recede and Jack suddenly focus on him.

"Daddy."

"That's right. Your Daddy. Just focus on me, Jack. Focus on my face."

Again he repeated the words until the fear faded from Jack's eyes.

"He's here, Daddy," Jack whispered. "He'll take me away."

"No," PJ said firmly. "No one is taking you away from me."

"You don't know what he's like."

PJ couldn't help his sad smile. "Little one, over the past year I've met some of the worst of humanity. I know exactly what your uncle is like. But I won't let him hurt you again."

Jack raised his fingers to stroke along PJ's cheek. "I want to believe you."

"What would make you believe me?"

Jack's expression hardened and there was little of his boy left in his face. "Throw the man off the edge of the mountain so he can't hurt anyone else."

PJ remembered the moment they'd thought Gruff had followed the CEO and the Hunter over the edge of the mountain to the ravine below. "How about we scare him off and if that doesn't work, we'll call the sheriff?"

Jack gave a curt nod. "He won't stop trying to get me."

PJ was never more grateful all his brothers were home. He had back-up to protect his boy. "He's not met me and my six brothers. You're not alone, little one." He wasn't sure

Jack believed him, but PJ would keep repeating it until Jack understood.

Reluctantly, PJ rose from the bed, not happy that his cock was softening without the pleasure of having buried it in his boy's body. "We need to get down there or they'll be coming to find us."

Jack rolled out of bed and headed toward the chest where PJ had made space for his clothes. PJ watched him, a frown between his eyes. Jack was shutting down and PJ didn't know why. He walked up behind Jack and pulled him against his front. He didn't like the way Jack tensed instead of melting in his arms as he usually did, but he held Jack in his beefy arms until his boy relaxed against him, his smooth back against PJ's furry chest and belly.

"I'm not gonna leave you, little one. You're my boy," he murmured in Jack's ear.

Jack gave a shuddering gasp. "I'm so lucky."

"I'm the lucky one," PJ assured him. "You've made my world."

Jack turned into PJ's chest and buried his face in his fur. PJ stroked his back in soothing circles. They could wait downstairs. His boy needed comfort.

The knock at the door wasn't a surprise. Jack pulled away, mopping his face.

"We're coming," PJ snapped.

"Hey, it's me. Can I have a word?" Alec said.

"Yeah, hold on." PJ looked at Jack. "You get dressed in the bathroom."

Jack took his clothes and disappeared into the bathroom, shutting the door behind him.

PJ flung on his robe and opened the door. "We're on our way down."

"I just want to talk to Jack," Alec said, and PJ noticed how grim his expression was.

PJ stepped back and Alec walked in and shut the door. PJ quickly dressed in a hoody and sweats. From the look on Alec's face, he needed to be dressed for this conversation.

"So this guy says he's Jack's uncle?" he asked, with a nod toward the closed door of the bathroom.

Alec nodded, showing PJ he'd gotten the message. "He looks like an older version of Jack. He says his name is Marty Large." Alec grimaced. "The guy is making my skin crawl and I don't know why."

Jack opened the bathroom door and stood hesitantly in the doorway. "You've got good instincts. My uncle is a criminal. Always has been. Monster's been in and out of prison since he was a teenager."

PJ reeled Jack into his arms, determined to keep him safe. "Monster?"

"I call him that," Jack muttered.

"He says he just wants to take you home to your gran," Alec said. As Jack pressed his lips into a thin line, Alec narrowed his eyes. "You don't believe that."

"Monster *will* throw me over the side of the mountain without a second thought." Jack saw Alec's eyes narrow. "You don't believe me? Look!" Jack wriggled from PJ's hold, picked up his phone from the nightstand, tapped the screen, and thrust it at Alec. Then he went back into PJ's arms. "He's dangerous."

PJ hadn't seen the messages, but when he saw Alec's face tighten, he knew they were bad.

"You know they're from him."

"I know."

"Why's he chased you halfway across the country?"

"I've got something Monster wants," Jack said grimly.

PJ narrowed his eyes. "What have you got?"

"I don't want to tell you. I don't want to put you in danger."

PJ knew Alec had seen far worse, but this was Jack, his brother's boy, his life. Alec would never laugh at his fear.

"I understand," Alec said gently. "I just want you to know I believe you, but it'll help if I know what he wants."

Jack looked between PJ and Alec, then shook his head. "I can't put my Daddy in danger."

PJ opened his mouth to protest, but Alec nodded. "PJ, step outside for a moment."

"Hell no," PJ roared. He wasn't letting Jack out of his sight.

Jack clung onto PJ's hoody. "Daddy, please. I can't let Monster hurt you."

PJ put his large hands over Jack's. "Have you seen the size of me?"

"You're twice his size but he's three times as nasty as you, Daddy." Jack reached up to press a kiss to PJ's lips. "Let me talk to your brother...I'm sorry, I can't remember your name."

Alec smiled at Jack. "I'm Alec. My brother, Jake, and I run a private investigation service. PJ, just stay outside the door. This'll take two minutes, tops. I promise you I'll help your boy."

PJ clenched his jaw. But he'd trusted his brothers all his life. He had to trust Alec now. He pulled Jack against him and gave him a long, lingering kiss, pleased to see Jack's eyes unfocused when he let him go. "Two minutes."

He stomped out of the bedroom and leaned against the closed door. He couldn't hear a word which frustrated him.

Matt emerged from the small room, wearing his jacket,

and a pack on his back. "Why have you got your ear to the door?"

PJ gave him the side-eye. "Why are you running away —again?"

"I'm not," Matt protested. Then he had the grace to blush because he plainly was. He let out a huff. "I need to get back to work. My boss has given me an ultimatum. Come back to work now or don't come back at all."

PJ wasn't entirely sure where Matt worked. "You could stay here," he pointed out. "Where you belong." He saw the sadness cross Matt's face. "He loves you, Matt."

"I know. And I love him. I always have. But I don't belong here. See you around, big man."

Matt gave him a wave and jogged down the stairs.

"You're an idiot," PJ muttered as the door opened behind him.

"Has he gone?" Alec asked. He sounded so miserable PJ wrapped him in his arms and hugged him close.

"You should go after him," PJ said.

"The more I chase, the more he runs away. One day he'll realize he can stop running and come home." Alec stayed in PJ's arms for a moment, before he said, "Let go of me, you big oaf."

PJ let him go with a final squeeze. "I want to meet this Monster."

Alec nodded. "But you let me take the lead, huh?"

"If he lays a finger on my boy..."

"He won't," Alec said confidently.

Jack slipped his hand into PJ's. PJ wanted to lock him in his bedroom and hide him forever, but he squeezed Jack's hand and they walked down the stairs. Jack let go of his hand as they walked into the kitchen. It was silent, which almost never happened.

PJ spotted Jack's uncle immediately. He was an older version of Jack just as Alec had said. Monster sat at the table with all Jack's brothers around him. He was either oblivious or indifferent to their glowering expressions.

"About time," Monster said as he spotted Jack. "It's time you came home, boy."

Jack shrank against PJ. "I *am* home."

PJ's heart swelled at his boy's declaration. He scowled at Monster. "You heard him. You can go now."

He watched Monster take a deep breath as though he were trying to calm himself.

"Your gran misses you, Jack. You don't want to make her unhappy, do you?"

PJ wondered if Monster thought anyone was buying the fake smile.

Jack shook his head. "You don't care about Gran. You never have. You just need somewhere to live."

"What the hell are you really here for?" PJ demanded.

"He's got something of mine and I'm not going without it," Monster snapped.

PJ looked down at Jack. "What have you got, little one?"

JACK

"These." Jack said. As everyone turned to look at him, Jack opened his fingers to reveal four large, dark seeds.

"Seeds?" PJ looked confused. "He chased you across the country for seeds?"

"They're beans," Jack said.

"Coffee beans," Monster snapped. "From Arabica cherries and eaten by elephants."

There was a long silence for a moment.

"You want him for elephant poop?" PJ demanded and burst out into a rumbling belly laugh.

Jack stared at him as if he'd lost his mind.

"These beans are priceless," Monster screamed. "Worth more money than idiot farmers like you can ever dream off. And he stole them from me."

"*You* stole them," Jack said, "And you were going to torture elephants to make this coffee. I heard you talking to your business associates. I took them so you couldn't hurt any creature and then I ran."

PJ sobered rapidly. "There are more priceless things than elephant poop, old man. Your nephew for one. Him, and boys like him, deserve to be cherished and loved." He smiled at Jack as though he were worth a hundred times the value of the beans. "Not used by you."

Tears prickled the back of Jack's eyes as PJ gave him a tender smile. He wanted to throw himself into PJ's arms. Then PJ held out his arms and Jack did just what he wanted, launching himself at PJ who enfolded Jack tight against his massive chest.

Out of the corner of Jack's eye, he spotted the exact moment his uncle understood, when the sneer crossed his lips. Jack pushed himself closer against PJ. His uncle was dangerous. What would be his next move?

"I won't let him hurt you, little one," PJ murmured in his ear. "Not for the most expensive elephant poop in the world."

Jack wanted to believe him. He really did. But even if his uncle did kill him, for a short time in his life Jack had been cherished and cared for. Jack would hold that to his heart for as long as it beat in his chest.

"It's time you left, Mr. Large," Alec said, distracting Monster's attention from Jack.

"Not without the beans and my nephew."

"I'm not going with you," Jack burst out.

Alec held out his hand. "Give me the beans, Jack."

Jack stared at him, betrayed. He clutched the beans to his chest.

PJ put his large hand over Jack's. "Give the beans to me, little one."

Jack's hand shook but he let his hand open and dropped the beans into PJ's hand because his Daddy asked him to.

PJ sighed and kissed the top of his head. "I love you."

He gave the beans to Alec who studied them for a moment. Jack tried not to feel betrayed, but those beans had been his only security.

"Where did you get your beans from, Mr. Large?"

"What's it got to do with you?" Monster snarled.

Alec's lip curled as he studied Monster. "Because these beans are protected. You stole these beans. You ain't getting them back."

Monster launched at him. Before he'd gone two steps, Jake stuck his leg out and Monster landed on the floor. PJ turned Jack in his arms so Monster couldn't get near him.

Alec and Jake picked Monster up.

"You need to leave, Large."

Jack jerked in PJ's arms thinking Alec meant him.

"Hush, little one, not you," PJ soothed. He held Jack tenderly and rocked him.

"I'm gonna kill you," Monster roared.

Jack's heart thumped in fear. He pressed hard into PJ who held him tight.

"Lay one finger on my boy and—" PJ started.

Alec held up his hands. "Leave it with me, PJ."

To Jack's surprise, PJ nodded. "Get him out of here."

Alec and Jake dragged Monster out of the kitchen, still bellowing at Jack. Jack's legs trembled.

"We're gonna sit down, little one," PJ murmured, guiding Jack over to the table and pushing him down.

Jack collapsed into a seat and PJ sat next to him. "What if he comes back and finds me again? He could take me from the bar."

"We'll stay with you if we have to," Gruff said.

"You can't do that," Jack said faintly.

"We'll do whatever is necessary to take care of our boys," Damien said, and the brothers all nodded.

Jack blinked back tears. "Thanks."

PJ mopped his eyes with a tissue. "I told you my brothers have your back."

The kitchen door opened, and Alec and Jake walked back in, twin looks of satisfaction on their faces.

"Has he gone?" Jack asked.

Alec came over to Jack, kneeling in front of him. "He's gone and he'll never bother you again."

"You don't know that."

"He's in custody. The Sheriff just took him away."

Jack blinked. "He's been arrested?"

"We called the sheriff's office as soon as he arrived," Alec said.

"Are they going to arrest me?" Jack asked, his voice wavering. "I stole the beans."

"You took them for the best possible reason. You're not going to be arrested. The sheriff wants to talk to you, but he knows you're staying with us. You're safe with PJ and us."

Jack couldn't hold back his tears and he burst into tears. Alec patted his shoulder and PJ dragged him onto his lap. Jack sobbed into PJ's shoulder. He was safe. He couldn't believe it. PJ rocked him again and they sat in the kitchen as everyone else faded away and left them alone.

Finally he was cried out and resting against PJ who gently stroked his head. He sighed and curled his fingers around PJ's flannel shirt. "I can't believe it's all over. I thought I was never going to get away from him. Will someone tell my gran? She'll be worried. She loved Monster." He growled a little. "She was the only one."

"Do you want to see your Gran again?" PJ asked. "She might appreciate your support."

"He got arrested because of me. She'll probably never want to talk to me again."

PJ handed Jack his phone. "Call her now."

"How did you get ahold of my phone."

"I'm sneaky like that," PJ smirked. "Now call your Gran and let her know you're alive."

Jack stared at the screen and then at PJ. "What if she doesn't want to talk to me?"

"Then you'll have me, six brothers, and four boys who want to love you."

"I've got nothing to worry about then." Jack gave a shaky laugh and scrolled down his contacts.

He listened to it ringing.

"Hello?"

"Gran?" Jack said shakily.

"Jack? Baby, is it you?"

Tears pricked Jack's eyes. "Hi, Gran."

"Did your uncle find you? He said he was going to look for you. Why did you run away?"

Jack shook his head. His gran was always the same. She was so blind to her only living son. "Gran, you need to listen to me. Monster's been arrested."

There was a long silence and Jack would have thought

the connection had been dropped, except he could hear the TV in the background, the continuous news cycle his Gran insisted on watching. She'd been a news junkie his entire life.

"Don't call him that. He's your Uncle Marty. Is it serious? Does he need me to post bail?"

Jack took a long breath. "Gran, he wants to kill me. Please don't post bail."

He expected her to protest, but she didn't say a word. "You knew."

She gave a long huff. *"I hoped he'd gotten over that stupid idea, but Marty's always been a troubled boy."*

Only his gran would think of his uncle as troubled. But did this mean he couldn't trust his Gran?

"I won't post bail, sweetie."

Jack breathed easier. "Thanks, Gran."

"When are you coming home?"

Jack had been really hoping she wasn't going to ask that question. "Not yet, Gran. I've gotten a job and...and...I've met someone." He felt PJ relax beside him. Was PJ worried Jack was going to walk? Jack smiled up at his Daddy.

"He's important to you."

Jack stiffened. "You know? You know I'm gay?"

His gran chuckled. *"I've known for a long time, sweetie."*

"You don't mind?"

"I love you. Why would I mind?"

Jack pressed into PJ. "I love you, Gran." He found it difficult to talk past the lump in his throat.

PJ took the cell phone out of his hand. "Hi there, Mrs. Large. My name is PJ, I'm Jack's boyfriend. Jack just needs a minute."

Jack listened to his boyfriend and his Gran talk while he calmed down. He never thought he'd have this day. PJ told her how he met Jack, and Jack heard her laughing and then saying she would shake her stick at him if he hurt her grandson again.

"I promise never to hurt him," PJ said solemnly. "Unless he asks me to," he mouthed at Jack.

Jack smirked and held his hand out for the phone. PJ handed it over. "Gran, I'll call you soon, okay?"

"Love you, son."

"I love you too, Gran. Bye."

Then Jack leaned against his Daddy and wondered when he'd gotten so lucky. PJ picked him up and gave him a tender smile. "We're going upstairs now, little one. We were interrupted earlier."

Jack wrapped his arms around PJ's neck and let his Daddy carry him upstairs.

10

PJ

"You're a beauty," PJ crooned to his old mare as he brushed along her back. "You know you are."

Bella huffed and nudged him, showing her love as she always had. She was a rangy, old quarter horse, just right for his size, and PJ had adored her from the moment he rescued her from an ex-customer of the farm. The second he saw the starving horse, he'd called the sheriff, loaded up Bella and brought her home to a better life. He'd refused to have anything to do with the customer ever again and his brothers had backed him.

PJ took his time brushing his horse, murmuring sweet nothings in her ear. She deserved all the love he could give her after a hard day working on the farm. They had ATVs too, but he loved the time wandering over the land on Bella. There wasn't an inch of the Brenner land he didn't know. He'd been born here, and he hoped he'd die here too.

PJ chewed on his bottom lip. What did his boy want? Before Jack, PJ had mapped out his life. Now Jack might want something different. He couldn't expect Jack to stay if he didn't want to. PJ had wanted to get a horse for Jack, but his boy spent too much time working at the bar to look for one. PJ had been trying to find a way to suggest to Jack that he quit his job at the bar because his boy was always tired. He knew Jack needed his independence, and Jack had given the money he earned from the bar to PJ for the old pickup. PJ had put the money into an account for Jack. The boy just didn't know it yet.

He sighed and rested his forehead against Bella's strong neck. "I want him to stay with me, Belle. Not spend all day fending off Daddies and Tops."

"Are you a Daddy or a mouse?" PJ muttered to himself. "Just go Daddy on his ass and tell him you want him to stay at home. Then spank his ass because it's so pretty when it blushes for you."

And Jack really liked being cheeky to his Daddy to get naughty spankings. PJ shivered as he remembered Jack crying and yelling and coming over his legs the previous night.

"Are you talking to Bella or yourself?" Harry asked.

PJ groaned and turned to see his brother leaning against the stall of Thunder, Damien's grumpy horse.

"How much did you hear?"

"Enough." Harry held out his hand for the brush. "I'll finish off with beautiful Bella. Your boy needs you right now."

"What's wrong?" PJ demanded, slapping the brush in his brother's hand.

"He's in the kitchen," Harry said, not answering PJ's question.

PJ jogged back to the cabin, panicking all the way. He knew if it had been serious, Harry wouldn't have looked so calm. But his boy needed him. That was all he could think of. His boy needed him.

He burst into the kitchen to see Jack on his own, staring at an envelope in the middle of the old family table. "Little one, what's wrong? Did something happen at the bar?"

"I walked out of the bar. I don't have a job," Jack said, not taking his eyes from the envelope.

"You did what?" PJ stared at Jack who refused to look at him. That worried PJ more than Jack's information.

"I kneed a guy who grabbed my ass. I took him down. He threatened to call the cops."

Flames exploded in PJ's head at the thought of some random dude grabbing his boy, even though the outcome was exactly what he'd wanted. Jack at home with him.

PJ sat next to Jack and took his hands. To his relief, Jack finally turned to look at him. He looked spaced out, rather than worried.

"You're not making much sense, boy. Tell me what happened."

Jack narrowed his eyes. "If you promise not to kill him."

"I'm not making any promises until you tell me what happened," PJ stated firmly.

"I was bussing the tables when one of the guys grabbed my ass and squeezed it. I'm so fucking tired of the customers thinking they can grab me." Jack huffed. "One minute I'm telling myself to calm down and the next, I kneed the guy in the balls."

PJ stared at him, wide-eyed. "You did?" Then he frowned. "How often do they assault you?"

"Down, Daddy," Jack said dryly. "I'm a bartender. It comes with the job."

"You're my boy," PJ said. "No one touches you without permission. No one. Why didn't Pablo throw the guy out?"

"He wasn't there. The new assistant manager was in charge."

From Jack's disgusted expression, he didn't think much of the new guy. PJ hadn't met him yet, but when he did PJ would have something to say to him.

"He tells us just to get on with it," Jack continued. "But this time, I kneed the guy, and he went down like a sack of potatoes." PJ couldn't miss the satisfaction in Jack's voice. "The guy called the cops but two of the Daddies backed me up and the cops left. The assistant manager was angry with me. He shouted at me, and I thought why am I doing this? So I told him to stuff his job and walked out."

PJ gathered Jack into his arms. "You did the right thing."

"PJ...Daddy...I haven't got a job now. I'm so sorry." Jack's voice was muffled in PJ's chest. "We can sell the pickup."

They'd probably have to pay to get the old pickup taken away, but that wasn't PJ's immediate concern. He cupped his boy's chin in his hands. "You don't need to pay me back for the pickup. And you don't need to worry about finding another job. Let me take care of you for a while."

"But—"

"Boy, I'm going to take care of you and you're going to be my boy." PJ's Daddy had had enough. If he had to order his boy to stay at home, he would. All the other boys had found their role in the Brenner household. So would Jack in time.

He watched the myriad of emotions pass through Jack's expressive eyes. His boy was scared. He didn't want to be dependent on his Daddy in case it exploded in his face.

"I will never leave you without money, little one." PJ stroked Jack's cheek. "If our relationship ends, then you will have somewhere to live and a job. You won't be on a bus with no money in your pocket."

The relief that went through Jack was visceral and he trembled. "Okay." He shuddered again. "Okay."

"I'll get something set up with our lawyer. A contract. Something to make this formal."

PJ had never had a relationship before. He had no real idea how to draw up a contract. He'd talk to his brothers and ask for their help.

"You don't have to," Jack said.

"Yes, I do," PJ assured him. "You and me. Daddy and boy."

"You're gonna shout at Pablo, aren't you?" Jack murmured.

"Yes." PJ was definitely going to shout at Pablo. And the assistant manager. And the handsy dude if he ever found out who it was.

"Good." Jack snuggled into PJ who rocked him tenderly.

"Why were you staring at an envelope?" PJ asked after a while.

"Elephant poop," Jack said.

"What?"

"I was staring at a pack of elephant poop that costs more than my pickup."

"Jack, you're not making sense."

"That coffee is made from the beans like I stole from my uncle. Alec gave it to me. It was thanks from the makers of the coffee for not letting my uncle's scheme go ahead. He wanted to steal the elephants. Where did he think he was going to keep them?"

PJ stared at the envelope of coffee. "Christ," he muttered. "Do we drink it or frame it?"

"We'll drink it at the right time," Jack said.

They both stared at it.

"You know we're never gonna drink it, don't you?" PJ said.

Jack snorted. "Why do you think I was staring at it for so long?"

PJ sighed, stood, and took the envelope and put it at the back of a cabinet. He needed something more than elephant poop coffee. "Let's go up to our room."

He loved how gracefully Jack switched into little mode. He held out his arms and swept Jack off his feet. Jack sighed happily and buried his face into the crook of PJ's neck.

At the top of the stairs, PJ heard voices and changed his mind. He walked down to the playroom.

Jack raised his head. "Daddy?"

"I need Daddy time too."

PJ eased Jack to the floor and knocked at the door.

"Hello?" Gruff said, sounding wary.

"It's PJ and Jack, could we come in to play?"

He was aware that the other Daddies and littles in the family had formed a bond while they were away. Maybe it was time he and Jack asked to join. But if they said no, he would take Jack into their bedroom and hope his boy wouldn't feel rejected. He would never intrude on their time.

The door opened and Lyle smiled at them shyly. "Come in."

JACK

Jack clung tightly to his Daddy's hand as they went into the playroom. He took one look at Lyle and Anna and tugged on his Daddy's hand.

PJ smiled down at him. "You want your new tiger onesie and your Binky, don't you?"

Jack nodded, suddenly looking shy.

"You sit down next to Lyle, little one, and I'll go fetch them."

"I'll look after you," Lyle promised, beckoning Jack to sit next to him.

Jack looked up at his Daddy who gave him a nod. Then he skipped over to Lyle. Anna gave him a shy smile. He knew it was hard for Aaron to get into her headspace, so he leaned forward and said "That's a pretty dress." It was a pretty blue with lace around the bottom.

Anna blushed and smiled at him, and earned a pleased smile from Gruff. He wasn't sure where Anna's Daddy was.

Jack heard a rumbling, "Good boy," behind him before PJ left the room.

Vinny was curled up with his Daddy in the big chair, reading a book. There was no sign of Matt. He hadn't seen him since the day Monster had turned up.

"Where's your Daddy?" he asked Anna.

"Daddy's working." Anna wrinkled her nose. "He wanted to be here, but he and Uncle Alec had to leave. Uncle Gruff promised to look after me."

Jack would have to ask his Daddy if he was supposed to call the others 'uncle' when he was a little.

His Daddy returned with his Binky which he handed to Jack, and his onesie. PJ patted the bed and Jack hopped up. He wasn't sure how he felt about being changed in front of everyone else, but no one paid any attention. His Daddy tugged his polo shirt over his head, then encouraged him to lay down on the bed. Daddy tugged his pants and briefs down and then put him into his tiger briefs. The second PJ snapped the final fastening of his onesie, Jack sunk fully into his little mode.

"I like tigers," Lyle confessed when he sat down on the

floor again.

"Me too," Anna said, "although I like lions best. Like Nala from the *Lion King.*"

Lyle wrinkled his nose. "She's a girl. I like boy lions like Simba with a big mane and a roar."

Anna's lip wobbled.

"Lyle," Gruff chided. "What did I say?"

Lyle huffed but he said "Sorry, Anna. Girl lions are as good as boy lions."

Jack looked away so he didn't laugh. Lyle sounded disgusted. Boy lions were much better than girl lions, although boy tigers were best of all.

He sucked on his pacifier as he played with the cars with Lyle and Anna. He knew he only had to lean back, and his Daddy would be behind him, holding him if he needed it. He could also feel how relaxed PJ was, sharing this time with his brothers.

Vinny joined them once he'd finished his book, but he was a bit bossy. His Daddy told him off and made him stand in the naughty corner. From the cuddle and kisses he got when he completed his punishment, Jack was sure Vinny had deliberately been naughty.

He was happy when Uncle Gruff produced snacks of cheese and chips and grapes. He'd missed his lunch driving back to the cabin.

When Jack was too tired to play, he crawled into his Daddy's lap and let PJ rock him. It had been a long day, especially once he kneed the mean man who grabbed him. He was sorry about losing the job, but he was more worried PJ was annoyed at him. Jack sighed, knowing he was losing his little headspace.

"Want to go to our bedroom, little one?" PJ asked.

"Please, Daddy. Me tired."

"Say thank you to Uncle Gruff for letting us join the playdate."

Jack gave Gruff a shy smile. "Thank you, Unca Gruff."

"You're welcome, Jack. You and your Daddy are always welcome to join us," Gruff said.

PJ picked him up and they went into their bedroom, PJ using his foot to close the door behind him. They curled up on the bed, PJ spooning around him.

"Let's have a nap, little one," PJ murmured. "We can worry about everything else when we wake up."

"Want fur," Jack grumbled.

PJ sat up and pulled off his hoody. Then he slid Jack out of his onesie. Jack sighed as he pressed back against his Daddy's furry body. Now it was perfect.

He closed his eyes. He wasn't really sleepy but he could doze while his Daddy napped. His Daddy was older and needed the sleep, after all.

———

"Hey, little one, do you want your dinner?"

Jack blinked sleepily at his Daddy. He hadn't realized he'd fallen asleep. "What time is it?"

"Nearly seven. Lyle just knocked on the door and said dinner is nearly ready."

"I'm not hungry," Jack admitted.

PJ ran a hand down Jack's back. "Pablo called. He wants to know when you're coming back to work."

"What did you tell him?"

"That my boy was staying at home with his Daddy, and you'd only be back as a customer."

Jack took a deep breath. "Was he cross?"

"Yeah," PJ admitted. "But not with you. I explained

what happened and said you were my lovely boy, and this was my decision." Then he smirked. "He called Aaron to see if he wanted the job back and he got Jake instead."

Jack grinned. "I guess he got the same response."

"Aaron wouldn't mind working there. I think he feels a bit out of place here. But Jake hit the roof. He doesn't trust Pablo after the guy fired his boy."

"I didn't like the job," Jack admitted. "I was going to ask Sheila if she had a job in the diner."

"You should have told me," PJ chided gently.

Jack looked away. "I didn't want to disappoint you."

"You never disappoint me, little one."

Jack rolled over and into PJ's arms. He pressed his mouth against his Daddy's. PJ groaned under his mouth and parted his lips. PJ pressed him down into the mattress and made love to Jack until he forgot about his shitty day and the strange coffee and his fear for the future.

After making love, Jack lay in PJ's arms. loving the feel of PJ's fur against his sensitized skin. Their legs were entangled, and Jack's hand rested over his Daddy's heart.

Jack raised his head to look down at PJ. "Can I work with you?"

"On the farm?" PJ asked, sounding puzzled.

"I wanted to ask before," Jack admitted. "But then everyone came home. What are they going to do?"

"I thought about this earlier. Gruff and Lyle and Damien and Vinny will be tied up with the Kingdom theme parks for years, along with Alec and Jake, and their boys. Gruff and Damien used to work on the farm. I wondered how I was going to cope with all the work." PJ stroked Jack's head. "It's not difficult work, but it's physical and you're working in all weathers. Are you sure you want to do that?"

Jack propped himself up on his elbow and looked down into his Daddy's face. "I want to do anything that means I'm close to you."

PJ looked up. "That works for me, little one. You and me, we'll run the farm. And if your Gran ever needs us, she can come here."

"I'm not sure how she'd cope with seven gay daddy bears," Jack admitted.

"Why don't you introduce us?" PJ suggested. "Let's see how she starts with one."

The End

Hello from Sue

Thank you for reading Jack's Giant. So, delayed by a year, but finally out is Boy Riding, Harry and Red's happy ever after.

Here's a teaser from their story.

They came in like avenging angels after Kingdom Water Theme Park closed for the evening. Men in various uniforms, others in black T-shirts, cargo pants, and more guns strapped to them than Red had ever seen, and hooded-eyed men dressed in dark suits and long coats, swarming in before anyone had a chance to run.

Red was rounded up along with the other boys and taken to the entrance to the park. He heard the words cops and Feds whispered between the boys. The first he knew, the second was a blank to him. He watched as the Green-coats, the men who had dictated his entire life, were arrested, and taken away in police vans.

Protesting loudly, the CEO who ran the theme park was forced into a van with no windows. As the doors on the van were slammed shut, the CEO, a man Red had only seen when there were issues, caught his eye. For some reason, the man's ice-cold and knowing gray gaze made a shiver run down his back.

"Don't worry about them, kid," a slender man said to him. He was maybe in his thirties, Red wasn't sure, but he had a weird accent. "They're going away for a long time."

Red turned to look at him. "What do you mean?"

"Cooper, you're needed." One of the cops waved at him.

The man raised his hand in response. "You've been rescued. Things can only get better now. Stay here." Then Cooper was gone, leaving Red staring after him.

A small group stood in the center of the chaos. They were an odd mixture of four men built like mountains, with bushy beards and deep blue eyes. It was clear they were related. With them were four younger, slender guys. It didn't take much to realize they were all couples, even the two standing further apart. He wondered if anyone else saw it or if it was only him.

Red noticed that everyone deferred to one of the smaller men. He was very young, with tousled, dark wavy hair, and an expression in his brown eyes as if he'd been to hell and back. Red recognized that expression. He'd seen it in all the boys in Kingdom over the years. All the men looked strained, but this one had the weight of the world on his shoulders.

A large guy with a stern expression, not a cop, maybe a Fed, approached the man. "We can't find any other boys, Lyle."

"How many did you find?" Lyle asked.

"One hundred." The large man grimaced and looked as

if he were about to hurl. "We found their tower. It's behind the waterfall. There were three barely alive and one dead."

Red furrowed his brow. Why did that man call it a tower? The boys here called it the dungeon. Then Red processed what the man had said, and he bent over, unsure if he would puke. He dragged in deep breaths, trying to quell his churning stomach.

He wondered which one of the boys had died. Four of them had been dragged away yesterday for trying to flee. They were fools. He'd told them it was a bad idea. No one absconded from Kingdom in a group. On their own, maybe. There had been boys who'd escaped over the years and not been returned. But the rumors of what the Greencoats did to you when they caught you was enough to deter most boys.

Red had never tried to escape. What was the point? He had nowhere else to go. He'd never lived outside. That's what he called it. Outside. He had no idea what existed beyond the electric fences. He knew people lived different lives than him, because he watched all the visitors, the kids having fun with their moms and dads, and the groups of kids around their age screaming and laughing. None of them saw him.

"I wonder who died," he murmured.

"I heard it was Jamie," one of the boys standing next to him said. He was a few years younger than Red. "A Greencoat got him."

"Damn," Red muttered.

Jamie had been someone he looked up to. But he'd been warned about the punishment as they all had and chosen to ignore it. Now he'd paid the price.

"What's going to happen to us now?" The boy looked worried.

"Hell knows. Whatever it is, it won't be good."

Nothing was ever good for the boys of Kingdom Water Park, and whatever was happening now, wouldn't be any different.

————

Constance looked over her shoulder. "We're nearly at your new home, Red. Just try harder to settle, yeah?"

She was his social worker, but she'd reached her limit with Red. He'd heard her say it often enough. Now she was giving him to someone else. Three months of trying to deal with Red had driven her to the brink of the precipice. She'd collected him from the local sheriff's office, shoved him in a car, and told him there would be a long drive ahead.

Red didn't care. He would be gone as soon as they turned their backs. No one could keep him locked up now. This was what? Foster home number five? Although this time it was different. They'd taken him out of state. Constance had warned him to behave on the journey or the cop with them would handcuff him. He was a solid, silent presence at Red's side.

The car started to slowly climb the mountain road, the driver obviously not confident as he drove at a snail's pace.

"Where am I going?" Red rasped, his stomach clenching at the narrow road and tight curves.

"See the lights?" Constance pointed through the windshield.

He peered out of the window and saw twinkling lights far up the mountain.

"That's where we're going," Constance said. "It's a Christmas tree farm."

"No!" Red barked, his fists clenched, his voice shaking

as he took in how high they had to go up the narrow road. "Turn back, find me somewhere else. I'm not going there."

"There's nowhere to turn around until we get there, kid," the driver said laconically.

The road went on and on and on.

"You can't keep me locked up forever," Red snapped.

Constance huffed. "Red, it's a foster home, not a prison."

"On top of a mountain."

"Lyle and his...family are good people."

Red leaped on the hesitation. "Family. What does that mean?"

"The Brenner brothers run the Christmas tree farm. They've lived on Kingdom Mountain their whole lives." She saw Red's eyes widen. "Oh yeah, this is where your water park got its name from. There was a theme park at the top of this mountain. Anyway, Lyle lives with his partner."

"You're giving me to a gay couple?"

The driver snorted but he didn't say anything.

Constance shot the driver an annoyed look, took a deep breath, and said, "Yes."

The driver barked out a laugh. "One couple? Try seven, kid."

"Seven couples?" Red croaked.

Constance's scowl grew deeper. "Lyle and his family are good men. Without them, we'd never have known about what was happening in the Kingdom theme parks. They don't need any homophobic attitude from you, young man."

Homophobic? That was a laugh.

"It was my home," Red muttered.

"You'll find a better one," she insisted. "Give Lyle a chance. And be kind to him. They've been through a lot."

Red stared out of the window, his lips pressed together in a thin line. They had no idea. No idea at all. He didn't care the brothers were gay. So was he. But he had no intention of telling anyone. His silence was one of the things that had kept him alive and unmolested in the water park. He knew about the chosen and the disappeared.

It took another hour before they reached the twinkling lights wrapped around a pine tree.

"We're here," the driver said unnecessarily. "Connie, we're gonna have to dump and run. I don't want to drive down in the dark."

Red glowered at him. He wasn't a goddamned package. The driver had a point though. It would be getting dark in a couple of hours. There was no way Red could get back down the mountain road to the nearest town now. He was stuck for at least one night.

The car pulled up outside a large cabin, with a wrap-around verandah. Red squinted at it. The building seemed to go on forever.

"How many kids do they have here?" he muttered.

Constance gave him the side-eye. "None. Just you. There are seven brothers, remember?"

As they got out of the car, a door opened, and three men jogged down the stoop. He recognized two of them from the raid on the water park. The smaller, dark-haired one had to be Lyle. He looked more relaxed than at the raid. The third one he didn't know. He had to be one of the Brenner brothers as he was the size of a barn, but he had bright red hair, almost as vivid as Red's.

The cop held Red's arm. "Stay here," he ordered.

Red scowled at him. "I ain't going anywhere."

The cop was unmoved.

Constance's relieved huff was loud. "Lyle, it's good to

see you again. Thanks for taking him in."

Lyle's smile was somewhat strained. "You obviously needed help."

She turned and beckoned to Red. "Red, come here. This is your new foster family."

Red didn't move. The cop gave him an ungentle shove and he only just kept his balance.

Lyle smiled at him. "Red, I'm Lyle. This is my partner, Gruff, and my...brother-in-law is probably easier...Harry. Welcome to our home."

Red said nothing.

"Well, I'll leave you to it," Constance said. "We want to get down the mountain while it's still daylight."

"Do you want an escort?" Harry asked.

"We should be fine." She turned to Red. "Bye, Red. Just stay put, yeah?"

Red said nothing and she sighed. Then she was gone with the silent cop.

Cowards! Running away from him.

"Come meet the others, Red."

Lyle didn't touch him, but kind of herded him into a large kitchen with a table surrounded by huge men. A small dog was sacked out in front of the range. It didn't stir at Red's appearance.

"I don't expect you to remember everyone's name," Lyle said with a chuckle. "But Damien is the oldest and the head of the household." He pointed to a large, broad-shouldered man with gray in his bushy beard who Red had seen at the raid. "You do what he says. The man mountain is PJ. He's the biggest and the middle one. You can ignore him." Lyle grinned at PJ's protest. "Gruff is the youngest and mine. If you feel ill, talk to Harry."

"That's me."

Red turned to see the flame-haired man standing behind him. Harry had the big bear look all the Brenners had.

"I also take care of the horses. You can find me in the stables."

Red nodded, although it was irrelevant to him. He would be gone as soon as they relaxed, and no one would find him again.

"We'll show you your room after dinner," Lyle assured him. "Sit here."

He sat Red in an empty seat and Harry sat next to him.

"I'm Matt," the young man said on the other side. He was vaguely familiar.

"I saw you at the water park," Red said, and Matt gave a curt nod.

Red looked at the large plate of shepherd's pie Lyle put in front of him with some dismay.

"It's okay," Lyle said soothingly. "Just eat what you can. Vinny and I are still getting used to three meals a day."

Lyle was right. The food was great. But he was used to one bowl of oatmeal a day. Red ate maybe a quarter, and he was full.

But Lyle just took it away without a word. "If you get hungry, you can ask me for food or help yourself to anything in the fridge."

"I'm not staying," Red declared.

"You have to stay for a while," Gruff said.

"I'm not staying, and you can't make me."

Suddenly all this...this... whatever was too much. Red bolted from the kitchen and stood at the bottom of the stairs, not sure where to go next. The rich food churned uneasily in his stomach. He had to get out of here. He had to.

READ MORE HERE

The Bearytales in the Woods final two books, Alec's and Brad's stories are on their way too.

Sign up for my newsletter for all Sue's news.

ALSO BY SUE BROWN

You can find all of Sue's books over at Amazon. Don't forget to sign up for her newsletter here.

ABOUT SUE BROWN

Cranky middle-aged author with an addiction for coffee, and a passion for romancing two guys. She loves her dog, she loves her kids, and she loves coffee; in which order very much depends on the time of day.

Come over and talk to Sue at:
Newsletter: http://bit.ly/SueBrownNews
Bookbub: https://www.bookbub.com/profile/sue-brown
Patreon: https://www.patreon.com/suebrownstories
Her website: http://www.suebrownstories.com/
Author group – Facebook: https://www.facebook.com/groups/suebrownstories/
Facebook: https://www.facebook.com/SueBrownsStories/
Email: sue@suebrownstories.com

Printed in Great Britain
by Amazon